OTTO PENZLER PRESENTS
AMERICAN MYSTERY CLASSICS

# MURDER BY
# THE CLOCK

RUFUS KING (1893–1966) served in World War I and lived in Buenos Aires for several years before returning to the United States to begin a writing career. He published stories throughout the 1920s in magazines before introducing series character, Lieutenant Valcour of the New York City Police Department, in his first novel, *Murder by the Clock* (1929). Valcour went on to star in eleven novels and two films.

KELLI STANLEY is the Macavity Award-winning creator of the Miranda Corbie series, literary noir novels set in 1940 San Francisco and featuring "one of crime's most arresting heroines" (*Library Journal*). She is also a Bruce Alexander Award and Golden Nugget Award winner, and a Shamus Award and Los Angeles Times Book Prize finalist.

T0284226

# MURDER BY THE CLOCK

## RUFUS KING

*Introduction by*
## KELLI STANLEY

## AMERICAN MYSTERY CLASSICS

*Penzler Publishers*
*New York*

Published in 2025 by Penzler Publishers
58 Warren Street, New York, NY 10007
penzlerpublishers.com

Distributed by W. W. Norton

Cover image: Andy Ross
Cover design: Mauricio Diaz

Paperback ISBN 978-1-61316-623-9
Hardcover ISBN 978-1-61316-622-2
eBook ISBN 978-1-61316-624-6

Library of Congress Control Number: 2024918142

Printed in the United States of America

9 8 7 6 5 4 3 2 1

# INTRODUCTION

1929 IS a year enshrined in history books if no longer in vivid, living memory. The most popular car was the Ford Model A; the average hourly wage for automobile assembly was about thirty-six cents. Herbert Hoover was president, the first Academy Awards ceremony was held at the Hollywood Roosevelt Hotel with 270 attendees, and MGM's *Broadway Melody* was the highest-grossing motion picture (and the first musical). Less than half of all homes boasted indoor plumbing, though over half had access to electricity. Ernest Hemingway published *A Farewell to Arms*; Dashiell Hammett released *Red Harvest* and *The Dain Curse*. Eleven years after the Armistice, Erich Maria Remarque's *All Quiet on the Western Front* captured the mood of a nation determined to avoid another war. "Tip-Toe Through the Tulips" was the number one song of the year.

It was still the roaring, rapturous twenties, full of gin, sin, sex, and high spirits. Prohibition was in full swing, but privation had been conquered by proficient bootlegging and the concomitant growth of organized crime. If the Valentine's Day Massacre in Chicago that year was salacious news, it was quickly drowned out by another speakeasy opening.

On April 29, Rufus King published his third novel, a mystery-thriller entitled *Murder by the Clock*. On September 3, the stock market hit a peak that wouldn't be equaled until 1952.

On October 29, Black Tuesday, the worst economic disaster in U.S. history struck. The Great Depression had begun.

The world was a significantly different place than it had been six months earlier.

Yet King and his third novel achieved continued success. A "Crime Club" selection, it was optioned for a film and, for a time, King himself was exported to Hollywood as a scriptwriter. Reviews were mostly positive (*The Brooklyn Daily Eagle* sniffed that it was "decidedly better written than the average detective story"); King's career proved long and the book itself was still in print in 1966, the year he died.

When I was asked to write this introduction, I'd never read Rufus King—but I was intrigued by the title and the organizing principle. I've always loved procedurals—from *Robinson Crusoe* to Sherlock Holmes—and while the tone of *Murder by the Clock* seemed akin to S.S. Van Dine's Philo Vance novels, the propulsive time frame (almost all the action takes place in one night) promised suspense and, well, fun. I'm happy to say it delivered both.

But who, exactly, was Rufus King? I like to understand the author I'm reading—after all, reading is the closest thing we have to a time machine, a peek into another person's mind and soul, albeit, in this case, through a fiction intended for entertainment.

Not much is definitely known about him beyond what reads like marketing hyperbole from publishers. His obituary claims he wrote more than fifty books (I can only tally twenty-six) and "many" magazine articles. Further research yielded more fruit. He wrote three plays: *Murder at the Vanities* (co-written with

Earl Carroll and produced in 1933; made into a pre-code film in 1934); *Invitation to a Murder* (adapted as a film entitled *The Hidden Hand* in 1942); and *I Want a Policeman!* (co-written with Milton Lazarus and produced in 1936). He also published seven more books by 1935 and was regularly serialized in the then lucrative magazine and newspaper markets. Indeed, these years—from 1929 to the mid-thirties—were his most prolific and successful, even as so many across the country were forever traumatized by the horrors of the Great Depression.

King's *Who's Who* entry in 1966 offers a few more tidbits. He was born in New York City, January 3, 1893; his father was a medical doctor. He graduated with a B.A. from Yale in 1914, and served with the New York Cavalry on the Mexican border in 1916 and with the 105th in France from 1916–1918. He was awarded the Conspicuous Service Cross.

A 1932 gossip column from the *Pasadena Post* claims he'd been a wireless operator in addition to a "cavalryman" and an "artilleryman"; a review of *The Lesser Antilles Case* from the *Kingston Whig Standard* in 1934 touts that King's wireless experience had been on "freighters and other ships" and that the author had "served in the Marine division of the New York police." The column goes on to hint that "a longer list might be made of the exciting adventures which he has gone through."

Both his *Who's Who* entry and contemporary newspaper articles mention his involvement with RKO and Paramount. He began with a bang, adapting *Murder by the Clock* for film in 1931 followed by *Murder at the Vanities* in '34 (today remembered more for its pre-code musical numbers and the singing of *To Tell the Truth* panelist Kitty Carlisle Hart). But even before *Murder by the Clock* catapulted him to the upper echelon of authorial success, two silent films had been made based on his

IV · KELLI STANLEY

stories. The first was *The Silent Command* (1923), featuring Bela Lugosi. King is credited with the story. The second was based on King's first novel, *North Star* (1925), a heroic dog story riffing Jack London, filmed with the same title in the same year. The movie starred a Rin-Tin-Tin lookalike and featured Clark Gable in a small role and Gary Cooper in an uncredited one.

King himself was the uncredited adaptor of a story not his own with *A Notorious Gentleman* (1935) and the credited author of the story behind a turgid cheapie from Universal, *Love Letters of a Star* (1936). When *Invitation to a Murder* (which, incidentally, had featured Gale Sondergaard and a young Humphrey Bogart on Broadway) was transposed to film as *The Hidden Hand* in 1942, King received credit as the author of the original play. He next wrote the script for a 1946 comedy-caper *White Tie and Tails* along with Charles Beakon—the film combined a serialized novel of King's, *Double Murder*, with Beakon's play *Dangerously Yours*. In 1947, Fritz Lang directed an adaptation of King's novel *Museum Piece No. Thirteen*. Retitled *Secrets Beyond the Door*, the film noir, which starred Joan Bennett, Michael Redgrave, and Anne Revere, represents the apogee of King's association with motion pictures.

He later moved to Florida and wrote and published stories centered there; while not as popular as he had been twenty years earlier, he was still successful with collections like *Malice in Wonderland* (1958). The fact that he was able to sustain a career through the upheavals of the Great Depression, World War II, and paranoid, reactive postwar America demonstrates his talent, work ethic, and a timelessness that has earned him the well-deserved appellation of "classic."

King was unmarried his entire life, and author Curtis Evans has pieced together convincing circumstantial research and textual analysis to suggest that the author was gay. Given the dangerously repressive period in which King lived, his personal reticence and the dearth of actual records (I am unaware of any archived manuscripts or papers that might yield conclusive evidence), such speculation must remain speculative until some intrepid scholar embarks upon a biography. Sexual and gender identity are nearly impossible to retroactively label without testimony from the individual in question. It is, however, helpful to keep in mind that King may have led a private life that was nonconforming and potentially dangerous because of contemporary laws. During his lifetime, self-masking was synonymous with self-preservation; the need for a closeted existence could be expected to manifest itself in his writing in various ways.

In fact, one of the elements I liked most about *Murder by the Clock* could be such a manifestation: the outsider status and self-isolation of its protagonist. Yes, the story is propulsively designed—a hallmark of material that was serialized, and this was serialized in *Red Book* before being published as a novel. And yes, the premise is intriguing and entertaining, a kind of locked room whodunit constrained both by time and place. But what sets it apart from many of its contemporaries is the nonconformist status of police lieutenant Valcour, the most successful and prolific of King's recurring protagonists.

Valcour may be plunged into a *Dragnet*-esque chapter structure built on hours and minutes (*9:24 P.M. – Hall Marks* [sic] *of Murder*, reads the header for Chapter II) but the *Dragnet* similarity ends there. Rather than what would become the standard trope of the stoic, hardworking, step-by-procedural-step police officer, Valcour is an introspective dreamer. Though the novel hops into other voices occasionally, his predominates. He stands apart, alone, and comments on other characters and on his own thoughts in a reverie of near-meta self-awareness and observation. He is as much a Greek Chorus commenting on life as he is a detective.

Some of these are humorous, as if to show us that Valcour (and his creator) are well-aware of an inherent silliness of the genre in which they are working:

> How pleasant it would be, he reflected, to come across the perfect imprint of a shoe, or a rubber or—What was it that was so popular at the moment?—of course: the footprint of a gorilla. The case would then be what was technically known as an open-and-shut one. He'd simply take the train for California and arrest Lon Chaney and—But enough.

Valcour is a liminal figure, living in a dream world of his own as well as a contemporary New York; he stands apart and back from the action even as he directs it. This emotional isolation and external commentary by the protagonist (and by projection, the author), is perhaps more understandable when contemplating King's sexuality: his "outsider" status from the supposedly polite society into which he is thrust is palpable.

> He knew her instinctively as one of life's misfits: complex to a note far beyond the common tune; essentially an individualist; essentially unhappy from an inevitable loneliness which is the lot of all who are banished within the narrow confines of their own complexity; a type he had seldom met, but of whose existence he was well aware.

The empathy evinced in the above paragraph is remarkable—

as though Valcour is commenting on a kindred spirit, not a suspect in a murder investigation.

According to a 1934 article in the *Tampa Bay Times*, King gave a talk to a freshman composition class on the subject of commercial writing. "It is not necessary," he said, "to have committed murder to write a murder story, but it is necessary to have hated so deeply that one feels the capacity and the ability to murder."

Whether this was Method writing before the Method became wider known in acting, or whether it was pure public relations, the quote is particularly jarring in the context of the dreamy Valcour and *Murder by the Clock*, and may serve to indicate just how deeply buried Rufus King's emotions actually were.

Other characters in the novel are well drawn: one in particular reminded me of Jessie Florian in Raymond Chandler's *Farewell, My Lovely*. King overall seems less interested in the plot (some elements stretch credulity) than in drawing interesting, compelling people and containing those portraits within the pitchable, saleable gimmick of the ticking clock and the constricted setting. The story veers from mystery to thriller by the conclusion, with proto-noir elements thrown in for good measure.

King grew tired of Valcour or at least pretended to. In a 1934 newspaper interview, he claimed "I loathe Lieutenant Valcour . . . he's the biggest ass in the world. I've tried to kill him several times. Someday I'll get rid of him."

By 1936, King and Valcour were on the wane. That dreamy introspection was only viable in a world as yet untouched by the ravages of the Dust Bowl, economic refugees, and hunger and homelessness entrenched across the country. Readers and film audiences were embracing rougher role models who didn't play by the same rules as Philo Vance or the good Lieutenant: real-life gangsters like Dillinger, celluloid criminals like Cagney's *Public Enemy* and Robinson's *Little Caesar*. Crime fiction was embracing the leaner, journalistic styles of Hammett and the noir thrillers of James M. Cain in the early to mid-thirties; it wouldn't be until 1939 and *The Big Sleep* when Chandler successfully mixed the vividness and immediacy of Hammett with the dreamy lyricism of the eternal PI outsider.

King kept publishing and kept serializing. According to a newspaper report, he fractured his skull in 1945. By 1948, a positive review of *Lethal Lady* in the *Daily News* labels it a "mystery story by an old-timer. Rufus King, the author, must have written a hundred such stories and nearly all are good." He moved from Rouse Point, New York, to Hollywood, Florida, and passed away February 13, 1966.

King was a talented writer and a sharp observer of the world around him. Crime fiction spans a multitude of subgenres and he played with many before they were codified by marketing departments and publishing conglomerates. I adored *Murder by the Clock* and Lieutenant Valcour's musings stayed with me long after I finished the book.

I'm looking forward to reading more Rufus King!

# CHAPTER I
## 8:37 *p. m.*—Spring 3100

MRS. ENDICOTT thought for a moment of simply dialling the operator and saying, "I want a policeman."

It was what the printed notices in the telephone directory urged one to do in case of an emergency. But it wasn't an emergency exactly, nor—still exactly—was it a policeman she wanted. She wanted a detective, or an inspector, or something; a man to whom she could explain her worry about Herbert, and who could do something about it if he agreed with her that Herbert was in danger.

Mrs. Endicott had never had any personal contact with the police. Whenever she thought about it at all she thought of the force as an efficient piece of machinery, the active parts of which one observed daily from one's motor as healthy and generally good-looking young men who controlled traffic. She knew that there was a patrolman whose beat carried him past their door. Upon thinking suddenly about it she realized that she had only seen this man twice or three times at most during the past year. She knew that Herbert always left a ten-dollar gold piece to be given him by one of the maids at Christmas, and a check for twenty dollars as a subscription to some enterprise vaguely designated as the "fund."

She wondered momentarily whether the police characters she had seen in various plays, while at the theatre with Herbert, were true to life. Most of the characters had been brutal, in spite of a pleasant tender-heartedness reluctantly betrayed toward the final curtain, and just at present she wanted quiet, competent understanding—not brutality.

It occurred to her that a private investigator might be better, but she was uncertain as to the extent of their official powers. She decided to rely on the police, because the police could do something if they agreed with her that something ought to be done.

Mrs. Endicott looked up the telephone number of police headquarters and dialled Spring 3100. She grew nervous while waiting.

"This is Mrs. Herbert Endicott speaking," she said, when an undeniably masculine voice answered. It was an impersonal, efficient voice with no overtones about it. "Will you please connect me with your detective department? . . . I beg your pardon? Oh." She gave the number of her house on East Sixty-third Street between Fifth and Madison avenues.

"This is Mrs. Herbert Endicott speaking," she began again, upon a second voice's saying, "Hello," "and I am worried about Mr. Endicott. I wonder whether you could send someone up to talk it over with me. . . . No, he hasn't disappeared. I know exactly where he has gone, but I have reason to believe that something might happen to him. . . . Yes, it's the Mr. Endicott who has been in the papers recently in connection with Wall Street. . . . Around in a few minutes? But I thought police headquarters were down on Centre Street. . . . They transferred the call to the precinct station? Really. . . . Oh, thank you."

Mrs. Endicott replaced the receiver on its hook. She felt distinctly impressed at the efficiency with which her request had been so instantly transferred to the place where it could be handled competently and with dispatch.

The living room where she had been telephoning was on the second floor of the house. She left it and went to her dressing room, which was toward the rear of a corridor on the same floor. She gave her appearance a preoccupied inspection before a pier glass. The soft and uneven lines of the jade chiffon of her dress would offer a satisfactory mask, she felt, for the nervous tenseness of her body. She renewed the red on her upper lip where she had been biting it. She returned to the living room, lighted a cigarette, and picked up a novel which she did not read.

She smoked three cigarettes.

Her sense of aloneness became stifling. The conceit grew upon her nervous condition that she had changed places with the furniture. She had become inanimate and the furniture endowed with attributes of life, as if her being were under the influence of some dispassionate regard by something that had no eyes with which to see. It was nonsense—nonsense. She never should have listened—at least not attentively—to that wretched old woman. She could very well just have given the appearance . . . one had to be polite . . .

Mrs. Endicott moved restlessly to one of the draped windows and stared down on the silent street. About her stretched the city of New York, and yet her environment could not have been quieter in some cabin in the woods. Not as quiet. Her memory swerved to that hellish week with Herbert in the forests outside of Copenhagen . . . what on earth *was* the name of that little watering place . . . Trollhättan?. . . No, that was in Sweden. Names never mattered. She looked up for a while at a slender slice of night sky horizoned by cornices across the street. It was heavy with stars that held her as if they were so many magic mediums arranged in heaven for the express purpose of granting her earthbound wishes. Wishes? She shrugged. She released the drapes, and they settled into place.

A maid opened the living-room door and came in.

"A lieutenant from the precinct station, madam."

"All right, Jane. Ask him to come up here. Did he give his name?"

"Lieutenant Valcour, madam, I think he said."

"Try and be more careful in the future about getting names."

"Yes, madam."

Mrs. Endicott lighted another cigarette. Her sense of having done the proper thing began to desert her in a rush. The police had a habit of finding things out—unexpected things, irrelevant to any matter on hand. She was sure of it, and wondered on what she based the knowledge: books, hearsay. She would have to be careful, but after all, a person with intelligence—— He was standing in the doorway.

"My maid," she said, "wasn't sure of your name. Is it Valcour?" She noticed with a sense of relief that he was not in uniform and that he had left his hat and overcoat downstairs. Mrs. Endicott had an aversion to discussing things which fringed on possible intimacies with people who were hatted and coated. He was a mild elderly man with features that were homely but not undistinguished, well dressed in tweed, and not smoking a cigar. He affected her with a quieting sense of reassurance.

"Valcour is correct, Mrs. Endicott. I happened to be leaving for home when your call was put in, so I stopped in personally instead of sending a detective as you suggested."

The faint trace of cultured precision in his speech made her suspect foreign origin. She was sensitive to voices, and while not exactly collecting them, they almost amounted with her to a hobby. They were an essential part in the attraction she felt toward certain people, and it would have been within the bounds of possibility for her to have fallen in love with a voice.

"You are of French origin, Lieutenant?"

"French-Canadian, Mrs. Endicott. I became naturalized twenty years ago."

She offered her hand. They sat down. Now that he was here she felt that the necessity for hurry had vanished; his air of official protection had erased it. She wondered how it would be best to begin: just where to plunge into the foggy mass that composed her worry.

Lieutenant Valcour accepted a cigarette and lighted it. He was agreeably impressed with Mrs. Endicott and with the room. Both were unusual, and the competent foundation in culture he had acquired at McGill University in his youth enabled him to place them at a proper evaluation. The furniture was low set in design and severely simple, the general effect one of spaciousness and repose oddly marred by a muted undernote of harshness. It was not bizarre. He suspected it, correctly, of being modernistic. Mrs. Endicott herself had the startlingly clear perfection of features one occasionally finds in blondes. He decided that her age centred on twenty-five. Beneath her authentic beauty—her face seemed planed in pale tones of pink ice—there would be a definite substrata of metal. He noted that the six cigarette butts crushed in the vermilion lacquered tray on a small table beside her chair had not been smoked beyond a few puffs each. A clock standing on the broad-shelved mantel of the fireplace struck nine.

"My husband," Mrs. Endicott said abruptly, "has been gone now exactly two hours."

Lieutenant Valcour smiled amiably and settled himself a little less formally in his chair. His manner presented itself to her as a freshly sponged slate upon which she could trace any markings that she might choose.

"He left here at seven o'clock this evening," Mrs. Endicott said, "to go to the apartment of a woman with whom he thinks he is in love. Her name is Marge Myles, and her apartment is on the Drive."

Lieutenant Valcour's smile seemed to offer both consolation and an apology.

"I'm afraid there isn't very much we can do for you," he said. "It's always private inquiry agents who handle work of that— well, of that rather delicate character."

"No—I haven't made myself plain." Mrs. Endicott's indeterminate thoughts began to crystallize. "I'm not looking for evidence to secure a divorce. This woman is nothing of any permanence, but I'm afraid of her—of what she might do to Herbert." Then she added, as if the simple statement in itself would insure his comprehension, "You see, I've seen her."

"With him?"

"Yes. They were lunching at the St. Regis. Herbert always was a fool about those things. She's foreign-looking—the Latin type." Mrs. Endicott felt the need for being meticulously explicit. "Her eyes are like the black holes you see in portraits of Spanish women. They're the entire face; everything else blurs into a nonessential whiteness. This woman's eyes are like that— like weapons. I know she's the sort who would kill if she got stirred up over something—got jealous or something. People do get jealous enough to kill," she ended.

"Frequently." Lieutenant Valcour stored away in his memory the broken nail on the little finger of Mrs. Endicott's left hand. The uniform perfection of detail in the rest of her appearance made it stand out jarringly. "This is all most unfortunate," he said sympathetically, "but I still doubt whether there is anything we could do. If there were only something definite—say a threat, for example—we'd be very glad to investigate it and to offer Mr. Endicott suitable protection."

Mrs. Endicott stood up. The abruptness of the movement spread the folds of chiffon that streamed from a bow on her left shoulder, and Lieutenant Valcour's deceptively indifferent eyes lingered on bruise marks that showed blue smears upon white skin before the chiffon fell back into place.

"Would you come with me to my husband's room?" Mrs. Endicott said.

"Certainly."

"There's something there I'd like to show you—to ask you what you think about it."

Lieutenant Valcour followed Mrs. Endicott along the corridor that led past her dressing room. A door beyond this opened into her bedroom, and directly across the corridor from it was the door to Endicott's room. The blank end of the corridor served as a wall for the bathroom, which connected the two bedrooms and turned them into a suite which ran the width of the rear of the house.

Lieutenant Valcour sensed a difference in the furnishings of Endicott's bedroom that set it at sharp variance with the other parts of the house that he had seen. It was done in heavy mahoganies that were antiquated rather than antique, and methodically centred in each panel of its gray-toned walls was a print of some painting by Maxfield Parrish. After a comprehensive glance around he felt as if he had already met Endicott. He had at least evolved a fairly accurate portrait of the man's sensibilities, if not of his physique. He thought that Endicott would be difficult: a clearly divided neighbouring of the physical and the ideal, assuredly conscious of the fitness of things—which would be responsible for his acquiescence in the tone of the rest of the house—but dominated by an inner stubbornness which faced ridicule in the maintaining of his private room at the level he had accepted as a standard years before. "That is his desk."

Mrs. Endicott indicated a flat-topped desk which was placed before one of the rear windows. A lemon-jacketed book with crumpled pages was lying on it as if it had been slammed there. Near the book was a scrap of paper. Lieutenant Valcour leaned down and stared at the paper without picking it up. On it was printed in pencil:

# BY THURSDAY OR—

He looked at Mrs. Endicott. She was evidently waiting for him to speak.

"To-day is Thursday," he said. "Might it not be simply a memorandum?"

"My husband doesn't print his memorandums, nor is it likely he would use a piece of paper torn from a paper bag." She added, to clinch her belief, "I can't imagine Herbert ever having a paper bag."

"Perhaps he bought something at some haberdasher's."

"The paper is too cheap. It's more like the sort they use at grocers' or small stationers'."

"So it is."

"And there's a crudeness about the printing. It's almost an intentional crudeness." Mrs. Endicott stared fixedly at Lieutenant Valcour. "It's the sort of printing you'd expect to find in a threat," she said.

"I have learned to find almost any sort of writing or material used for purposes of conveying a threat," Lieutenant Valcour said. "People who threaten are invariably unbalanced emotionally, if not actually mentally, and there is never any telling just what they will do. There was a case that recently came to my attention where a woman received a threat which had been engraved on excellent paper and enclosed in the conventional inner envelope one uses for formal announcements or invitations."

"Really."

"I'm not, by that, questioning your judgment in the matter of this note, Mrs. Endicott. It might quite well be a threat, as you think."

"There is nothing else apparent that it could be."

"When did you find it, Mrs. Endicott?"

"After my husband had left."

"Lying just about where it is now?"

"Exactly where it is now."

"I see. You didn't touch it then—just read it. I wonder why your husband left it there."

She looked at him almost impatiently. "I don't imagine he did leave it there—that is, purposely. It probably fell out from between the leaves when he slammed the book down."

"Has it occurred to you that we might call up this Marge Myles—but that's foolish. Of course you'd have thought of that."

He observed her obliquely as she answered.

"He'd never forgive me." Her gesture was faintly expressive of helplessness. "I'm not supposed to know anything about it."

"Of course. This menace, Mrs. Endicott, this danger that you are fearing, where do you think it lies?"

She became consciously vague. "The streets—indoors—out——"

"And you're basing it entirely upon this note?"

"Primarily. It's something concrete, at any rate. I think that he ought to have protection, and yet, if I did do anything about it, he'd put it down as spying."

"Well, if this note is a threat there is rarely only one, you know. I wonder whether we might find any others. I haven't the remotest justification for looking, but I'm willing to do so if you wish me to."

Mrs. Endicott grew curiously detached. "His papers are in the upper right-hand drawer," she said.

Lieutenant Valcour opened the drawer. It's contents were in a state of considerable confusion. It was not the sort of confusion which is the result of a cumulative addition of separate notes, letters, and sheets of paper, but a kind that exists when a normally orderly collection of papers has been milled around in suddenly.

"There's quite a mass of stuff here," he said. "It might be simpler to eliminate other possible places before tackling it. I must repeat again that I'll be exceeding any legal rights by doing so, but if you earnestly believe your husband is in danger I'd like to go through the pockets of his clothing."

"Pockets?"

"It's a much more usual place to find important things than you would imagine."

"His clothes are in that cupboard."

Mrs. Endicott indicated a door. Lieutenant Valcour went over and opened it. An electric light was automatically turned on in the ceiling. The large hulk of a man crumpled into one corner of the cupboard gave him a severe shock. The man was dead. He closed the door and faced Mrs. Endicott. He nodded toward the desk, on which a telephone was standing.

"I'm going to use that telephone for a few minutes," he said. "There's a message I want to put through. Also, please ring for your maid."

Mrs. Endicott's eyes widened a little. "There's something in the cupboard," she said.

"Ring for your maid, please."

She went past him and toward the cupboard door. He shrugged. The value of her reaction would offset the brutality of not stopping her. She opened the door and looked in. Her grip tightened on the knob.

"Then he didn't go out at seven," she said.

"No, Mrs. Endicott. He didn't go out at all."

# CHAPTER II

## 9:24 *p. m.*—Hall Marks of Murder

Lieutenant Valcour felt that the utter stillness of the room would overwhelm him. He—Mrs. Endicott—everything seemed to be taking its cue from death. He reached past Mrs. Endicott and touched the body's cheek. It was quite cold.

"Where is your room, Mrs. Endicott?"

He carefully pried her fingers from the knob of the cupboard door and then closed it.

"But you can't leave him in that cupboard."

Her voice held the toneless qualities of arrested emotion, as if the functioning of her nerve centres had stopped.

"We must leave him in there, Mrs. Endicott, until someone from the medical examiner's office has seen him. If you'll tell me the name of your family physician before you lie down——"

"Lie down—I? Lie down?"

"Yes, and rest. I'll call the doctor up on the possible chance that we're mistaken, only I'm quite certain, Mrs. Endicott, that we aren't."

She stumbled verbally in her rush. "Worth—Dr. Sanford

Worth—Calumet 876—it's 876 something—I know it perfectly well. I—it's in my book—come with me."

She seemed mechanically vitalized, and her movements were those of a nervous, jerky toy. She flung open a door adjacent to the cupboard. It led into a bathroom, the fittings of which were of coral-coloured porcelain. A door in the opposite wall led into her bedroom. She went immediately to a leather reference book beside a telephone near her bed.

"It's Calumet 8769," she said.

Her finger slipped in the dialling. Lieutenant Valcour gently took the instrument from her hands and put through the call.

"The office of Dr. Worth?" he said, when a woman's voice answered him. "This is the home of Mr. Herbert Endicott. I am Lieutenant Valcour of the police department. Mr. Endicott is dead. I would appreciate it if Dr. Worth would come here at once and consult with the medical examiner, and also attend to Mrs. Endicott. Thank you." He replaced the receiver.

"I haven't the slightest intention of collapsing, Lieutenant."

"We will need Dr. Worth anyway, Mrs. Endicott."

Lieutenant Valcour dialled the Central Office and, in a suddenly most efficient voice, gave the requisite information. He then called his own precinct station and told the sergeant at the desk to send over a detail of five men in uniform.

"The chief of the Homicide Bureau, the medical examiner, and some of my own men will be here presently," he said to Mrs. Endicott.

"And my husband has to stay in that cupboard until they come?"

"Unless Dr. Worth arrives first and disagrees with me that Mr. Endicott is dead."

"It's inhuman."

"Very, but there's a set routine for these cases that we have to observe. Is this the button you ring for your maid?"

He pressed a push button set in the wall at the head of the bed.

"Yes, but I don't want her."

"You may, and there's no harm in her being with you. I'm going to leave you in here for a little while, until the people we've telephoned for come."

"You insist on my staying in this room?"

"Heavens, no. Do anything you like, Mrs. Endicott, or that you feel will help you. As long," he added gently, "as you don't leave the house."

"Oh."

"You see we'll have to talk such a lot of things over, just as soon as the usual formalities are finished."

"It's rather terrible, isn't it?"

"Pretty terrible, Mrs. Endicott."

"So"—she mentally groped for a satisfactory word—"so conclusive."

It seemed a peculiar choice. Lieutenant Valcour sensed that it wasn't just Endicott's life alone which was concluded by death, but something else as well—such as an argument, perhaps, or a secret and bitter struggle. The precise significance was elusive, and he gave it up, or rather checked it within his memory in that compartment which already contained six barely smoked cigarette butts, a broken finger nail, bruise marks, and a note which, in view of the body, might safely be presumed to have been a threat.

A maid knocked on the door and came in. She stared speculatively for a curious second at Lieutenant Valcour.

"Madam rang?"

"No, Roberts. Lieutenant Valcour rang. Lieutenant Valcour is of the police."

Any sudden announcing of the police is always shocking. It is a prelude to so many unpleasant possibilities even in the lives of the most blameless. They are in a class with telegrams. Lieutenant Valcour noted that Roberts accepted his identity with nothing further than an almost imperceptible catching of breath. Mrs. Endicott's attitude puzzled him. It wasn't resentment, certainly, or any stretching at rudeness; such emotions seemed so utterly inconsequential at this moment when she must have been wrenched by a very severe shock. It reminded him of the aimless play of lightning clowning before the purposeful fury of a storm.

"Mrs. Endicott will explain things to you," he said. "Stay with her, please."

There lingered, as he went into the bathroom, a picture of the two women, separated by the distance of the room, standing quite still and staring at each other: Mrs. Endicott, young, exquisitely lovely looking—the other, older, quite implacable. The connection was absurd, but the effect remained of two antagonists in a strange encounter who are standing in their separate corners of a ring. He closed the bathroom door and slipped the catch. He turned on all the lights.

There was a single window. He parted muslin curtains and looked at a glazed lemon-coloured shade, especially along its hemmed bottom. There were some smudges at its centre that interested him. He believed that they had been made by a dirty thumb. He raised the shade and the lower sash of the window.

The night was clear and cold and windless. A shallow stone balcony ran the width of the rear of the house. It was for ornamentation rather than use, as to get onto it one had to straddle the window sill. Lieutenant Valcour did so, and stood looking down upon the dimly defined outlines of what, in spring, would bloom into a formal garden. He satisfied himself that there seemed no access to the balcony from the ground unless one used a ladder or were endowed with those special and fortunately rare qualities which transform an otherwise normal person into a human fly.

The house was five windows wide; the two on the right of the bathroom belonged to Mrs. Endicott's room, and the two on its left to her husband's. He flashed on his electric torch and examined all five sills. None showed a trace of recent passage, and there was no very good reason, he realized, why any of them should. They were clean, windswept, and smooth.

How pleasant it would be, he reflected, to come across the perfect imprint of a shoe, or a rubber, or—what was it that was so popular at the moment?—of course: the footprint of a gorilla. The case would then be what was technically known as an open-and-shut one. He'd simply take the train for California and arrest Lon Chaney, and——But enough.

And the floor itself on the balcony was smugly lacking in clues. He relinquished the keen sharp air, the star-heavy night and returned to the bathroom by way of its window, which he closed, and again drew down its lemon-coloured shade.

A cake of soap in a container set in the wall above a basin attracted his attention. It was so incredibly dirty. Someone with exceptionally dirty hands had used it and either hadn't bothered to rinse it off or else hadn't had the time to. The dirt had dried on it.

He couldn't vision such a condition of uncleanliness in connection with the hands of either Mr. or Mrs. Endicott, unless there had been some obscure reason. He preferred to think for the moment that the hands had belonged, and presumably still did, to the murderer. That, of course, eliminated the gorilla. What a pity it was, he reflected, that he was so constantly obsessed with infernal absurdities. Even though he tried to keep them under triple lock and key when working with his associates on the force, they had a distressing habit at times of cropping out into the open where they could be seen. Nor were they of a humour especially in vogue among his contemporaries; there rarely was an and-the-drummer-said-to-Mabel or an-Irishman-and-a-Jew among them. Rarely? He shuddered. Never. As a result there were occasions when he rested under the cloud of being considered mildly lunatic. It was bad business. He had told himself so firmly again and again. Success and humour formed bedfellows as agreeable as an absent-minded dog would be *en négligé* in the boudoir of a surprised cat.

With a beautiful access of gravity he lifted the lid of an enamelled wicker hamper and peered in at the soiled linen it contained. There were many towels. Towels were, he reflected, one of the few genuine hall marks of the rich. The Endicotts, hence, must be very, very rich, as it was obvious that they shed—or was it shedded?—towels as profusely as the petals fall from a white flowering tree.

There was a badly soiled and crumpled towel on the very top of the pile. He picked it up and looked at it. It was very dirty and still faintly damp. He folded it, set it on the floor beneath the basin, and placed the cake of soap upon it. They were, he smiled faintly, Exhibits B and C. The distinction of being classified as Exhibit A was already reserved by the threatening note on the desk. As for the smudges on the lemon-coloured shade, they would have to be definitely determined as finger prints before they could have their niche in the alphabet. The prosecuting attorney would be pleased. He was a man whose flair for alphabeted exhibits amounted to a passion. Lieutenant Valcour hoped that he could find a crushed rose. The prosecuting attorney was at his best with crushed roses. For example, take that knifing case in the Ghetto. Three petals were all the prosecuting attorney had had there, but they had bloomed, via the jury, into tears. Into tears, Lieutenant Valcour amended, and tripe.

A pair of silver-backed brushes showed no finger marks upon their shining surfaces, nor were there any on the silver rim that backed a comb. One could infer, Lieutenant Valcour decided, and did, that someone later than Mr. Endicott had used them, as Mr. Endicott would never have wiped them off to remove his prints, and had he not done so there certainly would have been some signs of usage. What a careful murderer it was, he thought, to polish the evidence so very clean. And what a grip the subject of finger prints maintained upon the criminal mind, and upon the lay mind as well. It seemed to embrace their Alpha and Omega in the scientific detection of crime. Lieutenant Valcour offered to bet himself his last nickel that the murderer had overlooked entirely the possibility of what might be found left within the bristles of the brushes and between the teeth of the comb. He took a clean hand towel from the rack and wrapped the brushes and the comb up in it. He set the bundle on the floor beside the cake of soap and the dirty towel. The alphabet, he reflected, had now been depleted down to F.

The bathroom could tell him nothing more. He reconstructed its segment of the drama before leaving it: the murderer had entered, gone at once to the window and pulled down its shade. There had been a washing of hands and a brushing and combing of hair. The murderer had wiped the silver clear of finger prints and had left. The whys and wherefors must come later. The shell would remain unchanged until the moment came to pour it full of motive and give it reason and life.

He went into Endicott's room and opened the cupboard door. The beam from his electric torch, added to the ceiling light, brought out sharply the waxy pallor of the face's skin. Its good-looking, homely ruggedness was marred by a slight cast of petulance, as inappropriate as a pink bow on a lion. Cruelty showed, too, a little—and something inscrutable that baffled analysis. Endicott weighed, Lieutenant Valcour decided, close upon two hundred pounds and no fat, either; a strong, powerfully muscled man, and about thirty-five years old. He played the light upon Endicott's right hand and exposed the wrist a little by drawing up the sleeve. The wrist and hand were normally clean, as he had expected.

He gently inserted his fingers into such of Endicott's pockets as he could reach without disturbing the body. From the rumpled state of their linings and their complete emptiness it was apparent that they had been hastily turned inside out and replaced.

Lieutenant Valcour began to sniff at a motive. Not robbery, exactly, in the ordinary sense, as an expensive platinum wrist watch and a set of black pearl shirt studs were untouched, but robbery in the extraordinary sense—one that had been indulged in for a certain definite purpose. He strongly began to suspect that there would be the ubiquitous "fatal papers." It might also develop that Endicott was the secretive owner of some fabulous jewel of a sort usually referred to as a Heart of Buddha, or perhaps some important slice of the Russian crown jewels—the number of which now almost equalled, he reflected, the thousands upon thousands of ancestors who came over to our shores on the *Mayflower.*

The top button was missing from Endicott's overcoat. It would have been torn away when the murderer had lifted his victim from the floor in order to drag him into the cupboard. Otherwise there wasn't anything that hinted at a struggle. There wasn't any blood, or any wound, or sign of contusion visible on the head, and no trace of blood around such parts of the cupboard that Lieutenant Valcour could see.

He suddenly wondered where Endicott's hat was. It wasn't on Endicott's head, nor in the cupboard, nor in the bedroom, which struck him as strange. He was a strong believer in the paraphrase that where the coat is, there the hat lies, too. One could look for it more carefully later. Just at present, of greater importance was Exhibit A.

Lieutenant Valcour went to the desk, picked up the note and studied it. The pencil used had been a thick leaded one, almost a crayon. And there, right before his nose in a shallow tray that held an assortment of office things, was a pencil with a very thick lead that was almost a crayon. He copied the note with it on the back of an envelope he took from his pocket. He compared the result with the printing on the note. They were alike.

One begins, he informed himself gently, to wonder.

# CHAPTER III
## 9:45 *p. m.*—Guards Are Stationed at the Doors

THERE ARE knocks, Lieutenant Valcour believed, and knocks. He ranged them from gentle careless rappings, through sly sinister taps, to imperative demands and, finally, thumps. He classified the ones at the moment being bestowed upon the hall door as official whacks. He was right. He put the scrap of paper and the crayon pencil in his pocket and turned to greet five men from the station house who flooded into the room on the heels of his "Come in."

They were intelligent-looking young men, well built, alert, and their uniforms were immaculate—five competent blue jays outlined sharply against gray walls. Lieutenant Valcour knew each one of them both by reputation and by name.

He nodded to the starchiest and youngest looking of them. "Cassidy," he said, "stay in here. O'Brian, stay by the front door, and keep Hansen with you to carry messages. There's a servants' entrance at the front, McGinnis. It's yours. And you, Stump, watch the door from the back of the house into the garden. If anyone wants to leave the house send him to me first. You can let anyone in, with the exception of reporters, and find out their business. Now in regard to the reporters just be your natural genial selves and say that apart from the plain statement that Mr. Herbert Endicott, the owner of this house, is dead and that—" Lieutenant Valcour choked slightly—"foul play is suspected, you can tell them nothing. The police, as usual, are actively on the job, have the case well in hand, and there is every reason to believe that in view of our customary efficiency the guilty parties will soon be brilliantly apprehended etcetera and so forth Amen. Excuse-it-please."

"Cuckoo," confided O'Brian to Hansen as, with Stump and McGinnis, they filed out.

"Cuckoo as a fox," agreed Hansen, who had worked under Lieutenant Valcour on a case before.

"Yeh?"

"Yeah."

Lieutenant Valcour and young Cassidy were alone.

"Tell me, Cassidy, how are the servants taking all this, if you bumped into any of them?"

"Sure, I only saw the girl at the front door, Lieutenant. She's a sorry piece, and was shivering worse than one of them new and indecent dances."

"Did she say anything?"

"She did not, beyond telling us to follow her upstairs. She took us to that door across the hallway first, and some lady said you was in here."

"How did that lady's voice sound to you, Cassidy?"

"Smooth, sir."

"Not nervous?"

"Devil a bit."

"What are you looking for, Cassidy?"

"The corpse, sir."

"It's in that cupboard."

"Is it now?" said Cassidy, casually removing himself as far from the cupboard door as he could. "It ain't one of them Western hammer murders, is it?"

"I don't know what kind of a homicide it is, Cassidy. There are no marks on him that I can see."

"Will it be poison, then?"

"Maybe."

"Well, let's hope it's one or the other. I hate them mystery cases where the deceased got his go-by from a Chinese blow gun, or some imported snake from Timbuctu, or parts adjacent."

"When did you ever work on such a case, Cassidy?"

"Sure, Lieutenant, you can read about them every week in the magazines. There's one that's in its fourth part now where some louse of foreign extraction kills a dumb cluck of a Wall Street magnet with a package of paper matches, the tips of which was so fixed that they exploded when struck, instead of acting decent like, and shot dabs of poison into the skin of his fingers. Can you imagine it? Just say the word and I'll bring it around to the station house and you can read it for yourself."

"Thanks, Cassidy."

"It'll be no trouble at all, Lieutenant."

An important knock on the door disclosed a stranger. Lieutenant Valcour addressed him, correctly, as Dr. Worth.

Dr. Sanforth Worth did not merely imagine that he cut a distinguished figure; he was sure of it. A certain grayness clung impressively about the temples of an intellectual brow, and he was probably one of the few physicians left in New York who had both the audacity and ability to wear a Vandyke. He was dressed in evening clothes and had not bothered to remove his overcoat or to give up his hat.

"Dr. Worth? I am Lieutenant Valcour, of the police. Mr. Endicott is in here."

Dr. Worth bowed gravely, and with a sparklingly manicured hand stroked his Vandyke once. "I have been afraid of something like this for quite a while, Lieutenant," he said. His voice, in company with everything else about him, sounded expensive.

Lieutenant Valcour raised his eyebrows. "It begins to seem, Doctor, as if everybody except Mr. Endicott himself anticipated his murder."

"Murder?"

It was Dr. Worth's eyebrows' turn. They raised. They fell. They became, in conjunction with pursed lips, judicious. He removed his overcoat and placed it, with his hat, upon a chair.

"I believe you will find, Lieutenant, that it is just his heart. His—— Dear God in heaven, man, what have you left him slumped down like this for?"

"You mustn't touch him, Doctor, unless you think he isn't dead."

Dr. Worth stiffened perceptibly. "Fancy that," he said. "Well, one would infer that he is dead, all right. Just the same, Lieutenant, is there any legal objection to opening his coat and shirt bosom? I dare say I could slit them, if you preferred. You see, it might be advisable to test for any trace of heart action with the stethoscope."

"I had no intention of offending you, Doctor. Go right ahead and do anything you think is absolutely essential to establish life or death."

Dr. Worth melted conservatively. "You see, sir, I know his heart. He had a nervous breakdown two years ago which left its action impaired." He loosened Endicott's overcoat and the black pearl studs set in a semi-soft shirt bosom. He listened for a moment, and then removed the stethoscope. "No trace," he said. "He's dead. Shall I button up the shirt front and the coat again?"

"It isn't necessary, Doctor."

The hall door opened abruptly. The homicide chief and the medical examiner came in, followed by a squad of detectives. Lieutenant Valcour was well acquainted with both officials. He introduced them to Dr. Worth and placed at their disposal such information as he had gained while waiting for them to arrive.

The department's experts automatically began to function at once. A photographer was already arranging his apparatus to make pictures of the body from as many angles as its position in the cupboard would permit. A finger-print man went about his duties along the lines laid down by established routine. The medical examiner and Dr. Worth gravitated naturally together and plunged into a discussion of Endicott's medical history.

The homicide chief, a well-built, alert-looking man of fifty, by the name of Andrews, drew Lieutenant Valcour a little to one side.

"What do you really make of it, Valcour?" he said.

"Oh, it's undoubtedly murder, Chief, but I doubt whether there'll even be an indictment unless we get a lucky breaks establish a definite motive, and get a confession."

"I feel that way about it, too. Any signs of an entry having been forced?"

"I haven't looked. I've been in here all the time, and my men just came."

"Well, Stevens and Larraby are making the rounds now. They'll let us know. If the autopsy doesn't show poison or some wound it'll be a nuisance. If it's a straight heart attack, as Dr. Worth claims, we might just as well drop it. Can you imagine getting up before a jury that's been shown a picture by the defense of a big husky like Endicott and saying, 'This man was scared to his death?' Suppose a woman was the defendant. They'd laugh the case out of court."

"Maybe it won't be as bad as all that, Chief. While you're busy in here I'll wander around and try to scare up something. Would you mind sending for me when the medical examiner reaches some decision as to the manner of death?"

"Sure thing, Valcour. I'll see to it, too, that those brushes and comb are looked into."

"I'll probably be in Mrs. Endicott's room. That's the door just across the corridor."

Andrews was aware of Lieutenant Valcour's reputation in the department for the painless extraction of useful information from people. "Go to it," he said. "And squeeze every drop that you can."

# CHAPTER IV
## 10:02 *p. m.*—Pale Flares the Darkness

Lieutenant Valcour wondered concerning Mrs. Endicott as he walked slowly across the corridor and knocked on the door of her room. A curious, curious woman, with youth and beauty that almost passed belief. He knew her instinctively as one of life's misfits: complex to a note far beyond the common tune; essentially an individualist; essentially unhappy from an inevitable loneliness which is the lot of all who are banished within the narrow confines of their own complexity; a type he had seldom met, but of whose existence he was well aware.

Roberts opened the door. The woman's face was butchered and her eyes had the quality of glass.

"Ask Mrs. Endicott, please, whether she feels strong enough to see me for a moment."

Mrs. Endicott's voice was definitely metallic. As it reached him in the corridor, disembodied from any visual association with herself, it seemed to hold a muted echo of brass bells.

"Certainly, come in. I wish, Lieutenant, you would give up the tiresome fiction that I am going to collapse. I'll ring, Roberts, when I want you."

"Yes, madam."

As Roberts passed him on her way to the door Lieutenant Valcour felt an imperative awareness of an attempt at revelations—an attempt to impart to him some special knowledge. Her eyes, as she glanced at him, lost their cobwebs and grew sharply informative. It was entirely an unconscious reaction on his part that forced from his lips the word "Later." The cobwebs reappeared. She left the room.

Lieutenant Valcour drew a chair close to the *chaise longue* upon which Mrs. Endicott was nervously lying. Flung across her knees was a robe of China silk, a black river bearing on its surface huge flowers done in silver and slashed at its fringes with the jade chiffon of her dress. He launched his campaign by first swinging, wordily, well wide of its ultimate objective. His tone, from a deliberate casual friendliness, was an anodyne to possible reservations, or fears.

"It is the tragedy of a detective's life," he said pleasantly, "that the sudden slender contact he has with a case affords such a useless background for human behaviour. You can see what I mean, Mrs. Endicott. Were I you, or some intimate friend either of yourself or of your husband, I would already be in possession of the countless little threads that have woven the pattern of Mr. Endicott's life for the past five or ten years. You'll forgive me for outraging oratory? It's a nasty habit I've contracted in later years whenever dealing with the abstract. I'm not making a speech, really. What I'm trying to express is that in that background, that pattern of Mr. Endicott's life, one thread or series of inter-related threads would stand out pretty plainly as the reason why someone should wish to kill him."

"I," said Mrs. Endicott, "have several times wished to kill him."

Lieutenant Valcour nodded. "There is nothing left for me but the trite things to say about marriage. And trite things, after all, are the true things, don't you think?"

"If they're just discovered. I mean by that, that to the person just discovering their deadly aptness they're true. Rather terribly so sometimes."

"But the aptness wears off with usage?"

Mrs. Endicott's slender hand and arm were models of quietness in motion as she reached for a cigarette. "Everything wears off with usage," she said. "Love quicker than anything else."

"But it doesn't wear off completely, love doesn't, ever."

Mrs. Endicott looked at him sharply. "Why are you a detective?" she said.

"The accident of birth—of environment. Only geniuses, you know, ever quite escape those two fatalities. My parents emigrated from France to Canada, where my father held a certain reputation in my present profession. My parents died. There was enough money to secure an education at McGill—one had contacts here in the States . . ." Lieutenant Valcour smiled infectiously. "I reversed Cæsar in that I came, was seen, was conquered."

Mrs. Endicott was amused. "How utterly conceited."

"Isn't it?"

The smile vanished from her face with the peculiar suddenness of some conjuring trick. She veered abruptly. "What are they doing in my husband's room now?" she said.

"Dr. Worth and the medical examiner are determining the cause of death." Lieutenant Valcour transferred his attention to a Sargent water colour above the mantel. "Dr. Worth has already expressed the opinion that it was heart failure," he said.

Mrs. Endicott offered no immediate comment. She withdrew, for a moment, into some private chamber, and her voice was rather expressionless when she spoke. "But that isn't murder."

"It could be—if the disease itself were used as a weapon."

"I don't believe that I understand."

"Why, if some person who knew that Mr. Endicott was subject to heart attacks were deliberately to shock or scare him suddenly, or even give him a not especially forceful blow over the heart, and he were to die as a result of any one of those things, that would be murder. It would have to be proved pretty conclusively, of course, that it had been done deliberately."

Mrs. Endicott joined him in his continued inspection of the Sargent. "It would indicate a rather circumscribed field for suspects, too, don't you think?"

"Yes. One would confine one's suspicions to those who were intimate enough with him to know of his physical condition. But apart from all that phase, there are those things we technically speak of as 'attendant circumstances.' They point to murder."

Their glances brushed for a second in passing and then parted.

"Such as?"

Lieutenant Valcour explained, with certain reservations. "The note you showed me—the position of Mr. Endicott in the cupboard—the fact that he is completely dressed for out of doors, but there is no trace of his hat—oh, several little things that speak quite plainly." He focussed her directly. "Where did Mr. Endicott usually keep his hats?"

"I've never noticed particularly. There's a cupboard downstairs in the entrance hall, and of course the one——"

"Yes, I've looked for it up here. I wonder whether you'd care to tell me what happened—what you did, I mean, and what you remember of Mr. Endicott's movements from the time, say, of his reaching home this afternoon."

Mrs. Endicott's face sought refuge in the very pith of candour. "Why, nothing much—nothing unusual."

Lieutenant Valcour laughed pleasantly. "That is where I fail in my background," he said. "The things done were usual to both of you and therefore of no importance. To me, however, they would prove interesting because of their unfamiliarity. Did you talk at all?"

"Elaborately."

"I beg your pardon?"

"I said elaborately. Herbert makes a point of talking elaborately whenever he's lying."

"I see—he was lying, then, about Marge Myles."

"And unoriginally. But Herbert never was original, much, in his emotions. He told me he was going to an impromptu reunion of some men in his class at the Yale Club. These reunions have occurred with astonishing regularity once a week for the past month, in spite of their impromptu character. I detest having my intelligence insulted," she ended, not unfiercely, "more than anything else in the world."

"You will forgive me for becoming personal, but I doubt whether Mr. Endicott understood you very well."

"He didn't understand me at all."

"And you, him?"

Mrs. Endicott momentarily disarranged the perfect arch of her eyebrows. "I could see through him perfectly," she said. "A child could see through him. But understand him? I don't think anyone could understand Herbert. He made a fetish of reticence. He was," she concluded, "half animal."

"And the other half rather cloudily complex?"

"A fog."

"And when he came home this afternoon at five?"

"Five-thirty—nearer six, even."

"Toward six, he joined you in the living room and gave you the weekly excuse."

"I didn't say the living room. It was the top floor—you may have noticed that this house has a peaked roof—in what would correspond in the country to an attic——" She stopped sharply, and her defensive veneer cracked for an instant, long enough to show that she was definitely startled. "I——"

"You feel that you shouldn't have told me that. Perhaps you shouldn't. If the fact of your having met Mr. Endicott in the attic has nothing to do with the case at all, it will cause us to snoop around among your personal affairs unnecessarily."

"He didn't 'meet' me there, as you say. He—I don't know why he came up there. I never will know why."

"You didn't ask him?"

Mrs. Endicott forced Lieutenant Valcour's full attention by the almost startling intentness of her eyes. "There has never been a direct question put or answered between Herbert and me during the whole period of our married or unmarried life," she said. "My hold on him was the static perfection of my features and a running, superficial smartness in attitude and mind that passed for intellect. His hold on me was that I loved him."

"Even when you wished to kill him?"

"I suppose even then. Mind you, I never wished him *dead*—there's a difference."

"Oh, quite." Lieutenant Valcour smiled engagingly. "You often felt like killing him, but you wanted it to stop right there."

"You know, I wish you'd come to tea sometime——" Mrs. Endicott's eyes contracted sharply. Her voice became a definite apology, not to Lieutenant Valcour, but as though its message were being sent along obscure and private channels to some port where it would find her husband. "There are moments," she said, "when you make me forget."

"Forgetting isn't a sin. That's natural. It's not loving—being mentally hurtful—that's a sin. There isn't any word exactly for what I mean. Did you both stay in the attic and go through the trunk together, or whatever it was you were going through?"

Mrs. Endicott smiled as if at some secret knowledge. "I wasn't going through a trunk," she said.

"No? I just mentioned it, as nine times out of ten that's what people do in attics."

"And the tenth customary thing," said Mrs. Endicott, reaching for a cigarette, "is suicide."

# CHAPTER V
## 10:17 *p. m.*—Living or Dead?

LIEUTENANT VALCOUR's eyes narrowed slightly. He had a habit of dividing suicides into two classes—those who talked about killing themselves, and those who did so. He knew that the two rarely overlapped. He felt a shocking conviction that in Mrs. Endicott's case she might well have been the exception which proved the rule. "I suppose an attic is the conventional place for suicide," he said. "Or at least to think about it."

Mrs. Endicott's laugh was without humour. "One doesn't need an attic in order to think about it."

"That's true. And so you went downstairs with him, then?"

"He followed me in here. That is," she corrected herself with noticeable carelessness, "we went into the living room and he wondered, while he kissed me, whether I'd mind very much being alone for dinner. I doubt whether you've ever experienced, Lieutenant, the rather perfect torture of a, well, an abstract kiss. Men don't."

"We're too self-centred, I'm afraid, or conceited or something, or else our sensibilities aren't refined enough to be hurt by it."

"But you could understand—if you could vision the background?"

"Everybody knows what love is, Mrs. Endicott."

"That's just it—it's the comparison of what is with what has been. It's an indescribably vulgar subject—kissing—but it's either very wonderful or very painful. People who claim it can be a combination talk nonsense. We can eliminate, of course—"

"Of course—'petting' they call it, or did. You never know from one minute to the next just what a thing is being called. And then he went to his room to dress?"

"Yes."

"Alone?"

"Certainly."

"Has he a valet?"

"Herbert? Heavens, no."

"And you dressed?"

"Yes."

"Roberts helped you?"

"Of course."

"Then when Mr. Endicott said good-bye?"

"He called it through the closed door."

Lieutenant Valcour almost visibly showed his surprise. "He did say good-bye?"

"Herbert insists upon saying good-bye. He rapped on the door and called in. If it would interest you to know his exact words," she said bitterly, "they were in the falsetto voice he uses when he thinks he's being especially funny and were, 'Don't be angry with Herbie-werbie, sweetheart. Goodie-byskie.'"

"They're almost a motive in themselves," said Lieutenant Valcour, smiling. "Which door did he rap on, Mrs. Endicott?"

"The hall door."

"I see. And you heard him going down the stairs?"

"One can't hear footsteps with the door closed."

"And that was at——?"

"The clock over there on my mantel was striking seven."

"And after that there is nothing further you can tell me about Mr. Endicott?"

"Nothing."

"You dined. You went to his room. You found the note. You began to worry, and then you called us up."

"That is it."

"Was it in this room here or up in the attic, Mrs. Endicott, that you told him you were going to kill him?"

"Here, after he—— That wasn't exactly fair, was it?"

"Heavens no, but awfully smart." Lieutenant Valcour's smile was the essence of pleasantness. "I do wish you'd continue with the 'after he.' After he did what? Or was it something he said?"

"Did."

"Yes?"

"I told you," she blazed, "that he was half animal. You can hardly expect me to become more explicit."

Lieutenant Valcour was genuinely upset. "I do beg your pardon, Mrs. Endicott," he said. "About this afternoon, were you in the house?"

"Partly. I had tea at the Ritz, early, about four-thirty—with," she added defiantly, "a man."

"Ah."

"Exactly so. That will permit you to reverse another tradition and go *cherchez l'homme.*"

Lieutenant Valcour found instant good humour. "So you decided to fight fire with fire," he said.

"If you care to call it that."

"Just who is Marge Myles, and what?" Lieutenant Valcour said suddenly.

"There are several terms one might apply to her. They all mean the same thing. I believe that recently, however," Mrs. Endicott said very distinctly, "she has lost her amateur standing."

"Recently?"

"The past year or so."

"Mr. Endicott had known her as long as that?"

"Until the past month or two my husband had not known her at all. He'd heard of her, of course, and so had I."

"Then she is a woman who once had position?"

"She was the wife of one of Herbert's friends, a man who died two years ago and left her penniless. They say, incidentally, that she killed him."

"Killed him?"

"It was just gossip, of course. They had a camp near some obscure lake up in Maine. The canoe they were in one evening upset. Harry Myles couldn't swim."

"And Marge Myles?"

"Marge Myles was famous for her swimming."

"Then the inference is that she, well, neglected to save her husband?"

"That—and that she deliberately upset the canoe. I repeat it's all gossip. People dropped him, you see, after he married her. That's a commentary for you."

"You mean they still accepted him while he was—that is, before the ceremony."

"Yes, while he was living with her. It's thoroughly natural, of course. People didn't have to recognize her then; they could ignore her. But you can't ignore a man's wife; you either have to

recognize her or not. The nots had it. If she had been a genuinely nice person, or an amusing one, I doubt whether the fact of
their having lived together really would have mattered. But she
wasn't."

"What was she before her marriage?"

"A member of that much-maligned group known as the chorus."

"And recently she had got in touch with your husband?"

"She looked up all of Harry's old friends. Don't you see? As
a widow she again had a standing—a shade higher, but similar
to the one she held before Harry married her. I don't know how
many others she landed, but she certainly landed Herbert."

"And you were afraid she would do something to him?"

"Well, she killed Harry."

"Then you personally believe the gossip?"

Mrs. Endicott did not bother to give a direct reply. She
shrugged, and twisted a little on the *chaise longue.*

"And do you associate her in any way, Mrs. Endicott, with
what has happened here to-night?"

She continued to evade further direct responsibility for an
opinion. "Who else?" she said.

"But the actual mechanics of it, Mrs. Endicott—how could
she have got into the house?"

"It could be done. Herbert himself might have let her in."

"That's going a little far, isn't it?"

"Yes. It was rotten of me to suggest it. I never really thought
it, Lieutenant. I just said it."

"And after all, Mrs. Endicott, why should she want to kill
your husband? You weren't trying to keep him from her."

"He might have been trying to keep himself from her."

"He might. It's stretching it a little, though, to think she'd deliberately kill him for that."

"She wouldn't do it deliberately."

"I don't know. When a woman starts out to kill she invariably chooses some weapon, or a poison. Every case has proved it again and again. But we're only speculating, aren't we? Who was it who took you to tea?"

"I haven't any intention of telling you."

"Because it might involve him?"

"He couldn't possibly be involved. If I thought he were I'd tell you in a minute."

Someone knocked on the door.

"Just the same, Mrs. Endicott, I wish you would tell me who he was."

"No."

Lieutenant Valcour was able not only to recognize finality, he could accept it. He considered Mrs. Endicott's very definite refusal to answer his question as of small consequence; there were so many more ways than one for frying an eel. He stood up and crossed to the door. He opened it and stepped into the corridor, closing the door behind him. Even in the dimmish light young Cassidy's normally ruddy face was the colour of chalk.

"What's happened, Cassidy?"

"Honest to God, Lieutenant, I'm scared stiff. They're getting things ready in there to bring that corpse back to life."

# CHAPTER VI
## 10:32 *p. m.*—Pictures in Dust

LIEUTENANT VALCOUR stared for a puzzled instant at the white face.

"What do you mean, Cassidy?" he said.

"Honest to God, Lieutenant, I mean just what I say."

"But that's impossible."

Cassidy went even further. "It's sacrilege," he said.

"Nonsense," Lieutenant Valcour said sharply. "You have simply misunderstood Dr. Worth. It is possible that Mr. Endicott was not dead at all but in some state of catalepsy. No one, Cassidy, can bring back the dead."

"I'm glad to hear you say so, sir."

"Then let us go in."

"Must I go back in there, too?"

"You must. Forget the fact that you're a superstitious Irishman, Cassidy, and remember that you're a cop. Cops, as you've been told more times than one, should be noble, firm, and perpetually cool, calm, and collected."

"Sure now, you're kidding."

"Tut, tut."

"Well, and I'll try, Lieutenant—but cripes!"

"But nothing," advised Lieutenant Valcour as he opened the door to Endicott's room.

The effect was shockingly garish. All shades had been removed from their lamps, and the various details of the furnishing stood out in the painful white light brightly clear.

Andrews was alone. He stood near the bed upon which Endicott had been placed, looking in rather shocked bewilderment at the body. Lieutenant Valcour joined him. A blanket had been drawn up to Endicott's chin, and the face which remained exposed looked very waxlike—very still—very much like a dead man's indeed.

"This is the damnedest thing, Valcour."

"What is, Chief?"

"They say there's a chance that this man isn't dead. Worth is going to operate."

"Operate? But Dr. Worth himself admitted that the heart had stopped beating after testing with a stethoscope. What sort of an operation?"

"Worth's going to inject adrenaline into the cardiac muscles."

"I wonder just how much value there is in that stuff."

"Well, unless Endicott's been poisoned, the medical examiner and Worth both seem to think there's a chance. They feel there's no harm in trying, anyway. It sounds silly to me, but they reminded me of that recent case in Queens—you probably read about it—where a man had been pronounced dead for six hours and was revived. Of course, they said he wasn't really dead, just as they now think that Endicott may not be really dead. No one can bring back the dead."

Lieutenant Valcour threw a bland look to Cassidy, who was standing in as convenient a position to the hall door as he could possibly get.

"They say," Andrews went on, "that adrenaline's been used off and on for years. Worth says they try it quite often when a baby is born 'dead.' Sometimes it starts the heart pumping and the baby lives."

Lieutenant Valcour shrugged. "It will make things pretty simple for us if it works with Endicott," he said. "He can make a statement and prefer charges himself. Where is everybody?"

"The medical examiner and Worth are downstairs telephoning and making arrangements for the operation. My men have finished and have gone back to headquarters. There wasn't any sign of forcing an entry, so it looks like an inside job, if there was any job. I tell you, Valcour, if it wasn't for your suggestion that robbery was a motive, or for that note that might have been a threat, I'd drop the whole thing. It's a different matter if the adrenaline doesn't work and an autopsy proves poison or something. Find out much from Mrs. Endicott?"

"Enough to be interested in learning more. Want the details?"

"Later, if I have to get to work on the case. You want to keep on handling it?"

"Yes."

"Go ahead. Call for any outside stuff you want us to check up on for you. I'll send you a report on the brushes and comb as soon as they finish with them downtown."

"You going, Chief?"

"No use in my sticking around, Valcour. We haven't a case yet, really, that calls for any Central Office work. Hell, according to those two six-syllable specialists downstairs, we haven't even got a corpse. Robbery there may have been, and it's your precinct—so go to it. I'll find out from the medical examiner when he gets back how the operation turned out, and if there's going to be an autopsy. If poisoning is proved and you haven't pinned it on anyone by then, I'll get on the job again. I suppose you'll see that the people in the house are given the onceover?"

"Certainly, Chief."

"I'll run along then. Good luck, Valcour."

"Thank you, Chief."

Andrews left the room and closed the door.

"I bet he's got a date," said Cassidy.

"He'd stay here if he had twenty dates, if he thought it was necessary," said Lieutenant Valcour.

"Well, I wish I had a date."

"You'll have a whole vacation if you don't brace up. I'm going to take a look in that cupboard, now that Endicott's no longer in it."

Even a cupboard seemed preferable to Cassidy to being in the room. "Can't I help you, sir?" he said with almost fervent politeness.

"No, Cassidy, you can't. You can stay just where you are."

"Oh, very well, sir."

Lieutenant Valcour picked up a straight-backed chair and took it into the cupboard with him. He held a sincere respect for the Central Office men, but at the same time felt that their work was too methodically routine to permit their darting along interesting tangents or wasting their time in strolls along bypaths that might lead to fertile fields. There was no criticism in his mind at all. He admired the system that had been established, and the expert functioning of its units and departments. He knew very well that its average of successes was greater than its average of failures. But it was deficient in that elusive, time-taking, and sometimes expensive thing known as the "personal equation." It remained, at its best, a machine.

A certain amount of carelessness, too, ran in the general plan. In many cases some things were slurred over, some missed entirely. This again was not surprising when one considered that the personnel was recruited largely from the more intelligent men in the ranks. Intelligent, yes, but hardly specialists, nor could one in all fairness expect them to be.

When working on a case they functioned along two distinctly separate but parallel lines. One department of specialists handled the technical and chemical investigation of material things and clues found on the scene of the crime—just as the brushes and comb were shortly to be examined by the proper men down at Central Office. A second department dealt with the human aspect—examining witnesses, looking up all friends or connections of the victim; a large, competent organization that would stretch feelers, no matter how many were necessary, to every contact point of the victim's life within the city, and from whose findings some possible motive could be established and some possible suspect or group of suspects be evolved.

The two branches would then compare notes, and if a satisfactory amount of evidence had been obtained by the technical department to establish a case against one or several of the suspects, arrests would be made or the suspects brought in for questioning. According to the temperament and station of the suspects, one of the various forms that go to make up the properly dreaded third degree would be employed and a confession obtained. The work of the Central Office would then be finished, and the case up to the prosecutor.

Lieutenant Valcour was glad that in the present instance

the homicide chief had felt it useless to set in motion the machinery of the second branch until more definite developments should occur. The case interested him. Mrs. Endicott interested him—her astonishing beauty, her mind, her contradictions—Roberts—Marge Myles—three women who offered an assurance of satisfying an almost blatant curiosity he possessed for discovering the source springs of human behaviour. This talk about reviving Endicott and Endicott himself making a statement—well, perhaps. But until it was accomplished he preferred to think of Endicott as a corpse, the case a definite homicide, and of possible suspects right in the house.

Lieutenant Valcour concentrated his attention upon the cupboard. There were shelves along the back of it, the lowest one being at the height of a man's head. Numerous suits of clothes were hanging from beneath this lowest shelf. He stood on the chair and played his flashlight along the top of it. There was nothing there but an accumulation of dust. He felt a distinct and highly satisfactory thrill when he noted that streaks showed where the dust had very recently been rubbed away, as if somebody had deliberately wiped both his hands in it. It linked with the dirty cake of soap. Andrews had said nothing about the streaks. It was pretty obvious that the Central Office men had overlooked them—had casually observed that the shelves were empty and had let the matter go at that.

Lieutenant Valcour began to feel quite pleasant and informed himself gravely that a deduction was in order. For a happy moment he considered the possibility of that curious and sinister Oriental influence that crops up so perennially in the very finest of murder cases—of Cassidy's murder cases: that elusive figure swathed in gray, whitely turbanned above coffee-coloured skin, who has a penchant toward religious fanaticism the esoteric rites of which involve dust. This breath-shocking villain would ultimately be trapped by the bright detective through the wretch's occult passion for this dust. Had one, Lieutenant Valcour wanted to know, such an enigma to deal with here? No, he informed himself sternly, one knew damned well one had not. But in the place of such a handy and beautiful deduction—what?

He stared at the dust and began to see pictures in it: a crouching person tormented by hate or fear, or both, who knows that Endicott is going to open the cupboard door. What, in the name of the lighter humorists, to do? The person dreads recognition. Is there no disguise? No, curse it—but yes—the dust! The person's hands are smeared, and by means of the hands, the face . . .

"Ain't there *nothing* I can do for you, Lieutenant?"

Lieutenant Valcour sighed and got down from the chair.

"Yes, Cassidy," he said. "You can take this chair and put it over by the hall door. Then you can sit down."

"Very well, Lieutenant," said Cassidy bitterly. "But when you're in that cupboard there ain't nobody in the room with me but that live corpse."

"Then sit where you can't see it."

"Cripes, Lieutenant, I don't *have* to see it. I get the chills just thinking about it."

"You'll get the gate, Cassidy, if you don't snap out of it."

"All right, sir, but if you come out and find me keeled over, don't blame me."

"I wouldn't dream of it, Cassidy."

Lieutenant Valcour reentered the cupboard. He examined the corner in which Endicott had been slumped. The suits on the hangers had fallen back a little into shape. He carefully went through their various pockets. They were empty, and from the rumpled condition of their linings he knew that they had been hastily gone through before. Perhaps the Central Office men had done so, but he doubted it. They would concern themselves pretty exclusively with the effects taken from the clothes Endicott had been wearing at the time of the attack.

It interested him to note that the suits against which Endicott's body had been slumped showed evidence of having been searched with the rest. It confirmed his theory that that was what the attacker had been doing when caught in the cupboard by Endicott's sudden appearance in the bedroom, and it also strengthened his theory of the ingenious use of dust from the shelf top as a disguise.

Shoes lined a low shelf along the bottom of one side, and hat boxes occupied a corresponding shelf on the other. Lieutenant Valcour dismissed the possibility that the particular hat he was searching for—the one that Endicott was wearing or intended to get at the moment of the attack—would be in a box. Perhaps it was in the cupboard Mrs. Endicott spoke about downstairs in the entrance hall. The point kept nagging at him irritatingly, and he considered it important enough to go down and find out.

Cassidy barely restrained himself from clutching Lieutenant Valcour's arm by the hall door.

"Honest to God, you ain't going to leave me in here alone, Lieutenant?"

"Honest to God, Cassidy, I am."

Lieutenant Valcour went out. Cassidy took one bleak look at his charge, the living corpse, carefully crossed the fingers of both his hands, and sat down.

"I just knew," he muttered truculently, "that this case was going to be one of them printed damn things."

# CHAPTER VII
## 11:01 *p. m.*—Banked Fires

THE CORRIDOR was deserted.

Lieutenant Valcour walked along it to the top of the stair well and looked down into the entrance hall. He could see the broad athletic back of Officer O'Brian on guard at the door. O'Brian's snub nose was pressed against the plate glass, and his eyes, one presumed, were staring out through the door's bronze grille upon the street.

As Lieutenant Valcour went down he wondered at the complete stillness of the house. There was no sound of any nature at all. There was a waiting quality about the stillness: a definite waiting for something that would shatter the hush into bedlam.

"What are you pressing your nose against the glass for, O'Brian?" he said.

The young policeman turned and grinned at him broadly.

"Sure, it's them boys from the papers, sir," he said. "They're all stirred up over what the medical examiner has just told them."

Lieutenant Valcour groaned faintly. "When was this, O'Brian?"

"Not two whisks of a lamb's tail ago, sir—out there in the vestibule."

"Did the medical examiner go out into the vestibule?"

"He did that, Lieutenant, and the last mother's son of them has just beaten it off down the street like a jumping jack rabbit. They were crazy after photographs, but he drew the line at that now."

"Really?" Lieutenant Valcour was politely astounded.

"Sure and he did—with the exception of a flash or two he let them take of himself."

"And were you the little birdie, O'Brian?"

"Was I the which, Lieutenant?"

"Did you say 'peet-tweet' over his left shoulder as the flashlights went off?"

"Ah, sure now, sir, and I did have the door open a wee bit. I was just explaining to the boys that they couldn't come in without your permission nohow, and it was then that the medical examiner came along and, hearing the talking, went outside to pacify them."

"A modern martyr throwing himself to the lions. Except for the tea party, O'Brian, has anything happened down here?"

"Not a thing, sir."

"Any of the servants been drifting around?"

"Only one old dame in black, and seven foot tall if she's one inch. She came halfway down the stairs, took one dirty look at me, and then stalked back up as stiff as a poker. Her bonnet was on her head."

"You don't know who she was, I suppose?"

"That and I don't, sir. She looked like she might be a housekeeper."

"She probably was. By the way, O'Brian, just what was it the medical examiner told the boys?"

"Lieutenant, I could make neither the head nor the tail out of it. I'd been telling them myself that the boss upstairs was dead and that foul play was suspected, and they were hot after the medical examiner for a further word, and I'm damned if he didn't give it to them."

"What was the word, O'Brian?"

"Indeed and it sounded like crinoline, sir—the stuff the missus do be talking about in old dresses."

"Was that all he said?"

"It was enough, sir. 'Crinoline,' said he, and looked very wise at that. Then he added, 'For the present, boys, no more,' and off they scampered like the devil in person was after them."

"All right, O'Brian. Just stick where you are."

Lieutenant Valcour wandered around the entrance hall but encountered, beyond his own and the medical examiner's, no hat. He knew that Dr. Worth's was still upstairs where the doctor had left it in Endicott's bedroom. He found the cupboard Mrs. Endicott had referred to. There was no hat. The subject was becoming a fixed idea. It was growing increasingly believable that the attacker had taken the hat and worn it out of the house. But why should the attacker leave the house? And what was the matter with the attacker's own hat? Time, if not Endicott himself, would have to tell.

From a reception room opening off the entrance hall he caught the murmur of Dr. Worth's and the medical examiner's voices in consultation. He passed the door indifferently and went upstairs.

. . . an old dame in black, seven foot tall if she was an inch. Her bonnet was on her head.

MURDER BY THE CLOCK · 51

. . . and her bonnet, Lieutenant Valcour repeated softly to himself, was on her head.

He continued on up a second flight of stairs to the third floor. A door toward the end of the hall was open, and light flooded out through the doorway. He walked to it and looked in.

A tall, thin woman sat on a chair before a grate in which some coals burned bleakly. She was unbelievably gaunt—her silhouette a pencil, rigidly supporting an austere face beneath a smooth inverted cup of steel gray hair. Black taffeta sheathed her, tightly pressing against flat narrow planes, and smoothly surfacing two pipelike arms that ended in the tapering, sensitive hands of an emotional ascetic.

Lieutenant Valcour rapped on the door jamb.

The woman did not start. Her head alone turned and faced him, and her eyes were a contradiction of nature—black planets glowing coldly in a sky of white.

"Pardon me, I am Lieutenant Valcour of the police. Are you, by any chance, the housekeeper?"

Her voice was of New England—low almost to huskiness, a trifle harsh, and completely stripped of all nuances.

"Yes, Lieutenant. I am Mrs. Siddons."

"May I come in? Thank you—please don't get up. I'll only stay a minute or two, if you don't mind."

He took a chair and placed it before the fireplace beside her own. He sat down and did nothing beyond observing obliquely for a moment the curiously artificial placidity of Mrs. Siddons's clasped hands.

"There is no use in questioning me, Lieutenant, because I have nothing to say."

Her tone was the chill clear winds that sweep the rigorous mountains of Vermont.

Lieutenant Valcour warmed his hands before the lazy coals and smiled amiably. "And I," he said, "have absolutely nothing to ask."

"That is a lie."

There was nothing abusive in the remark. It was simply a statement of fact, coldly, dispassionately pronounced by the remarkable pencil dressed in black who spired beside him. Lieutenant Valcour was shocked into a nervous laugh. He discarded his mask of indifference and stared at Mrs. Siddons openly and with complete interest. Not planets, her eyes—rather were they banked fires beneath whose ash hot coals smouldered deeply.

"I shouldn't wonder," he said, "but that your forbears came from Salem."

A look of interest stirred sleepily in the coals.

"Why so, sir?"

"Because there's a look of witch-burning in your eyes."

Mrs. Siddons gestured a slow negation.

"I would never abrogate the rights of God."

"But you would approve, Mrs. Siddons."

"I would *rejoice,* sir, in the crushing out of any evil or"—her tone became implacably stern—"of any evil thing."

"Or even of a human being?"

Her look did not waver.

"Yes, Lieutenant—or even of a human being." She went on steadily and unemotionally. Her words were fragments of stone chipped from some elemental quarry of granitelike conviction and harsh purpose. "That is why you find me dry-eyed, sir, in spite of the tragedy which has been visited upon this house."

Lieutenant Valcour felt that there was a catch in it somewhere. If she held Endicott's condition in the light of a tragedy then she scarcely regarded his death as an act of vengeance on the part of her unquestionably inflexible god.

"Tragedy?" he repeated softly.

"A tragedy, sir, for blinded eyes."

He hoped that she wasn't going to be allegorical. He endeavoured to interpret. "It is hard on Mrs. Endicott," he said.

For a moment he thought she was going to melt. "That poor young thing," she said, and her voice fringed on unaccustomed softnesses. "That sweet young child of beauty—what a bitter ending for the journey of her tormented heart."

He stepped delicately out upon the fragile ice. "But she's really better off, don't you think?"

"She will never know to the full the fortune of her release." Mrs. Siddons's incredibly thin body was suddenly shaken with passion as she added, "From that hateful—that filthy beast."

"Oh, come, Mrs. Siddons—no man is quite as bad as all that."

Her eyes blazed with the heat of a strange malevolence. "You didn't know him, Lieutenant, as we did."

"'We,' Mrs. Siddons?"

"Myself, sir, and the servants under my charge."

"You found him disagreeable—overbearing?"

Mrs. Siddons stared fixedly at the coals, as if finding in their vibrant reds some adequate illustration of her angered thoughts, "I found him such a man, Lieutenant, that I am glad to know that he is dead."

"But you see, Mrs. Siddons, he isn't dead."

He thought for a minute that she was going to faint and instinctively leaned forward to support her. She stood up unsteadily but refused the offer of his hands.

"If you will pardon me, sir, I believe I will lie down. There has naturally been a certain strain—a——"

She bowed and found her way to a door that led into an inner room. Lieutenant Valcour listened for a moment at its panels after she had closed it.

He could not determine whether the muffled sound he heard was of peculiar laughter or a sob.

# CHAPTER VIII
## 11:28 *p. m.*—Mrs. Endicott Screams

THE TANGENTS and the bypaths were beginning to increase. Lieutenant Valcour tabulated them as he went thoughtfully down the stairs and along the corridor toward Endicott's room: Mrs. Endicott herself, and the Spartan Mrs. Siddons—both had been partially explored; Roberts, with her astonishing glance that had hinted so definitely at revelations. Then what of Marge Myles? And what of the unknown man with whom Mrs. Endicott, that afternoon, had taken tea? He opened the door to Endicott's room and went in.

Preparations for the operation were practically complete. Dr. Worth and the medical examiner were beside the bed, and hovering near them were two trained nurses in uniform—middle-aged, competent women, starched and abstract looking, moving a bit aloofly in their private world which was so concisely separated from the sphere of laymen.

Cassidy, who seemed bleaker than ever, still stiffly occupied the chair near the doorway. He continued to inspect with an almost feverish interest an unsullied expanse of white ceiling above his head.

Lieutenant Valcour seated himself on the corner of a long mahogany chest that was placed before the window farthest from the bed and gravely watched Dr. Worth. He began to feel a little sickish and hoped that he wasn't going to make an ass of himself and faint. He had witnessed any number of accidents and stabbings, but had never been present at an operation, and it worked on his nerves. Even if Endicott weren't dead, he certainly looked it. Suspended animation and catalepsy were all right as figures of speech, but the human illustration was rather ghastly. Lieutenant Valcour felt justified in believing that he knew his corpses. He wondered why Dr. Worth was delaying—hesitating—no, bending over now, and in his hand, ready to give the injection of adrenaline into the cardiac muscles, was . . .

The response was immediate.

With the aid of the stethoscope Dr. Worth heard Endicott's heart throbbing again, growing steadily stronger. Quite noticeably beneath the bright white lights a faint flush started to run through Endicott's skin. Lieutenant Valcour saw it, and he moistened with his tongue the dry pressed surface of his lips.

Dr. Worth straightened up and handed the stethoscope to the medical examiner. "Endicott lives," he said.

No one had noticed Mrs. Endicott standing in the doorway. No one had even noticed that the door was open. It was her terrific scream, her dropping to the floor, that shocked everyone into instant awareness of her presence. Dr. Worth nodded to one of the nurses. With her aid he lifted Mrs. Endicott and carried her from the room. Everyone else remained quite literally spellbound, still chained within the influence of that extraordinary scream. It didn't seem more than a second or two before Dr. Worth returned. He went directly to Lieutenant Valcour.

"I have given Mrs. Endicott a narcotic that will keep her quiet for the night," he said. "It was outrageous—her being here. That guard at the door should have seen to it that it was kept closed."

"Most outrageous, Dr. Worth. I believe all of us were hypnotized by watching you."

"And I don't care what the law is, she can't be questioned or disturbed in any way at all until I say so."

"But that *is* the law, Doctor. You are quite within your rights to dictate concerning your patient."

"I don't want to dictate. I'm just as willing as anybody to have the criminal side of this mess cleared up, if there is a criminal side."

"Endicott would hardly have crawled into a cupboard to have a stroke, would he, Doctor?"

"No." Dr. Worth's intelligent eyes stared speculatively at Lieutenant Valcour for a minute. "Not unless he'd hidden in there to overhear something, and did overhear something that gave him a stroke," he said.

The cesspool, Lieutenant Valcour decided, was beginning to show strange depths within its depth. The medical examiner came over and joined them. He complimented Dr. Worth briefly on the success of his operation, assured Lieutenant Valcour that the homicide chief would be given a full report of Endicott's recovery, and presumed that from now on the case would be left in Lieutenant Valcour's hands. Lieutenant Valcour would deal with whatever charges of robbery or assault might develop from it. He said good-bye and left the room, with the fullest intention of going right straight home to bed; and so he promptly did, as soon as he had made the promised report to Andrews.

Dr. Worth pointedly raised his eyebrows. "Then there will be charges, Lieutenant?"

"That will depend largely upon Endicott, Doctor. As he is now revived he will tell us himself who attacked him, or the nature of the circumstance that gave him the shock."

"I trust so."

"There isn't any doubt, is there?"

Dr. Worth grew expansive. "Certainly there is a doubt," he said. "While it is true that Endicott has been revived, it is impossible to state definitely that he will recover consciousness. And even granting that he should recover consciousness, there is also a chance that he might prefer not to make any statement at all. What would you do then, Lieutenant?"

"Fold my tents, Doctor, and fade away."

Dr. Worth looked down a long straight nose for a minute at tips of low patent-leather shoes. "And if Endicott does not recover consciousness," he said softly, "what will you do then?"

"You'll be surprised at the number of things I will do then."

Dr. Worth's eyes, surfeited with patent leather, snapped up sharply. "I must impress on you that Mrs. Endicott is not to be disturbed," he said.

"She won't be, Doctor."

"Nurse Vickers, who helped me into her room with her, is going to stay with Mrs. Endicott all night. Two day nurses will come in the morning: one for her, if necessary, and surely one for Endicott. I need scarcely impress upon you the seriousness of *his* condition." Dr. Worth made a gesture of irritated bewilderment. "I wish I knew him more intimately—who his friends are, I mean."

"He never talked with you about them?"

"Never. He seems an unusually reticent man, with an almost abnormally developed feeling for privacy concerning his intimate affairs." Dr. Worth's manner grew definitely severe. Mentally, he wagged a finger under Lieutenant Valcour's nose. "He mustn't have any further shock. There must be nothing, absolutely nothing that will shock him when, and if, he regains consciousness." He directed his attention momentarily to the nurse. "Get those shades back on the lamps, please, Miss Murrow, and turn out the ceiling lights. And now, Lieutenant, to continue about Endicott. As she is under the influence of the narcotic I gave her, it is out of the question that his wife be here. I wish she could be. I want the first person he sees to be someone he knows—loves. His mind, you see, will pick up functioning at the precise second where it left off—at least, such is my conclusion."

"And that was one of shock."

"Yes, Lieutenant, evidently one of shock or of great fear. We cannot overestimate the importance of getting him past it safely. Personally, I shall sleep here in the house to-night, and Nurse Murrow will call me if Endicott shows any signs of coming to. That may not be before morning. I hope so, in a way, as the effect of the narcotic will have worn off by then, and Mrs. Endicott can be in here with him."

"One of the servants might know of some friend," Lieutenant Valcour suggested. "I take it you would like a friend to sit here with him during the night?"

Dr. Worth was emphatic. "It is almost a necessity that there should be. The mental and nervous viewpoints, you see, predominate in the case."

"There is just one thing that I would like to arrange, too, Doctor."

"Yes?"

"I want to keep a couple of men posted all night in the bathroom. They can sit on chairs just inside the doorway there, where they can watch the bed, but where Endicott can't see them. He need never know they are there."

"What on earth would be the need for that?"

"Why, it's quite simple, Doctor. When Endicott comes to he will be in a position to tell us who gave him the shock—a shock sufficient almost to kill him—one which would have killed him if we hadn't found him to-night—and if," he added thoughtfully, "Mrs. Endicott hadn't had her suspicions."

"But why the men in the bathroom?"

"Because I don't want to take any chances of there being a repetition before Endicott makes his statement."

Dr. Worth pursed his lips and looked very wise indeed. "I see," he said. "I see. You are afraid that the same person might get at him again and, well, silence him before he could talk."

"Something like that, Doctor." Lieutenant Valcour became courteously formal. "As the physician in charge of this case, sir, have you any objection to my stationing the two men in the bathroom?"

"Providing Endicott isn't able to see them and won't be disturbed by them in any way at all."

"Then that's settled. You'll have a nurse in here all the time, I suppose?"

"Naturally."

"Then I'm going to ask her to keep this hall door locked on the inside. She can open it if anyone knocks, and my men will keep their eyes on whoever comes in."

"The precautions seem extraordinary, Lieutenant."

"And so does the case. I'll go downstairs now and try to find out something from the servants about his friends. I'll tell them, if you like, about your staying here, in case there is anything that has to be got ready."

"Thank you, Lieutenant."

"Not at all, Doctor."

Lieutenant Valcour went outside. He found the maid Jane in the hallway, seated on a chair near the stairs, trembling. A tray with an empty glass was on the floor beside her. She saw him, picked up the tray, and stood up.

"I'm that upset, sir," she said, "*that* upset."

"Something has startled you?"

"Startled! Glory be, sir—what with this bringing back of the dead and the missus gone into a coma—if it wasn't for them three cops at the downstairs doors I'd be out of this house this minute, and so would the rest of us, too."

"How many of the 'rest of you' are there?"

"Sure and including the housekeeper there's eight of us, sir."

The Endicotts, Lieutenant Valcour was now quite certain, must be multimillionaires.

"All women?"

"Except for the houseman and chauffeur."

"And do they sleep in the house?"

"The chauffeur does not, sir. He has an apartment for himself and his wife and his three-year-old child, named Katie, over the garage in East Sixty-sixth Street, sir."

"Have all of you been in service here a long time?"

"Indeed and we haven't, sir—except for Roberts and the housekeeper. I've been here a month myself, and the rest of us not more than two or three."

"And Roberts has been Mrs. Endicott's maid for the past several years, say?"

"And sure and ever since she landed here from England, sir."

"Roberts is an Englishwoman?"

"Hold your whisht, sir, and I'll tell you that she's of the aristocracy, no less."

Lieutenant Valcour considered this gravely. It was not improbable. Many English families were utterly wrecked financially by the war, and the children had scattered whither they could, like sparrows, in search of bread. "You're sure of this?" he said.

"And indeed it is common knowledge, sir. The housekeeper herself, it was, who told me."

Lieutenant Valcour switched suddenly. "I wonder whether you could tell me who Mr. Endicott's intimate friends were," he said.

"Well, sir, there's quite a few people have called on the madam off and on, and a few on Mr. Endicott, too. I couldn't say, though, as to just how intimate."

"But didn't he ever discuss his friends?"

"Not before me, sir. I'm one of the downstairs girls. Perhaps Roberts would know. She's often in the room with the madam and Mr. Endicott even when the pair of them is quarrelling that hard that—— Glory be to——"

"Tut, tut," said Lieutenant Valcour gently. "Married couples are always quarrelling together. There's nothing unusual in that."

"Indeed and there ain't."

"I wonder whether you'd ask Roberts to come out here and see me."

"I will, sir."

"Oh—and will you also tell whoever has to know about it that Dr. Worth plans to stay here all night? And then let him know, please, where he is to sleep."

"Yes, sir."

Jane went to the door of Mrs. Endicott's room and knocked. Nurse Vickers opened it and stepped halfway out, blocking the entrance. Their voices were too low for Lieutenant Valcour to hear, but he saw the nurse retreat into the room, caught an affirmative nod from Jane, and presently Roberts came out and toward him.

"You wished to see me, Lieutenant?"

There was still that curious shielding in her eyes—a hinting at definite information kept closely guarded behind twin gates.

"I want you to tell me," he said quietly, "why you compelled me a while ago in Mrs. Endicott's room to say 'Later.'"

"I don't believe I quite understand."

"And I believe that you do."

Roberts became coolly detached. "One is justified in having one's beliefs."

"Just why do you hate Mrs. Endicott so?"

She flinched as if he had struck her physically.

"Is that why you sent for me?" she said.

Lieutenant Valcour himself indulged in a veiling of eyes. "I wish," he said, "that you would sit down."

# CHAPTER IX
## 11:55 *p. m.*—Queer Deeps

ROBERTS WENT indifferently to the chair that Jane had been using and sat down. Lieutenant Valcour drew another up beside her. He began with the usual distant skirmishing before launching the main body of his attack.

"I will explain why I wanted to see you," he said. "It's concerning Mr. Endicott—concerning his condition." He noted the sudden reflex from tension on the part of her hands as he summed up concisely the statement made to him by Dr. Worth. "I understand," he concluded, "that Mrs. Endicott is under the influence of a narcotic and will not be available before to-morrow morning at the earliest. Dr. Worth naturally wants to prevent all risk, and so we've turned to you."

He felt her staring through him, as if by some fourth-dimensional process his being had been erased from her vision.

"Mr. Endicott has very few friends," she said.

"You are taking the word at its literal meaning."

"Oh, quite. His acquaintances are numerous and transient." She focussed him into an entity again. "They are mostly women. I don't suppose one of them would do?"

Lieutenant Valcour smiled slightly. "Not if their status is so uncertain—their emotional status, I mean."

"Exactly." The masked effect of her attitude remained unchanged as she asked with almost perfunctory detachment, "Would a man do?"

"Why not?"

"Because there is one man of whom Mr. Endicott speaks quite frequently as being his 'best' friend."

"Here in town?"

"In a bachelor apartment on East Fifty-second Street."

"You have his exact address?"

"It is in the memorandum book beside the telephone in Mrs. Endicott's room."

Lieutenant Valcour grew markedly casual. "A mutual friend, then?"

"One couldn't say."

"He is your only suggestion?"

"He is the only man to whom I have heard Mr. Endicott refer in terms of friendship and of intimacy."

"Then there really isn't any choice."

Roberts' smile signified nothing. "No choice."

"Have you ever seen this man?"

"His name is Mr. Thomas Hollander. I have never seen him."

"Has anyone in the household ever seen him, to your knowledge?"

"I dare say. I don't know. One could inquire."

Lieutenant Valcour recognized the rising inflection at each period mark, a habit so much in vogue among certain types of English people when they wish to be mildly disagreeable. He felt a Gallic insistence to retaliate even at the expense of chivalry. At the worst, he thought, he would only be living up to the popular conception of the men in his profession. And there *was* some link of peculiar intimacy between this woman and Endicott. . . .

"If we cannot get hold of Mr. Hollander," he said, "would you consider it advisable for the post to be taken by yourself?"

He repented instantly at the sight of her deadly whiteness. It seemed impossible that blood could drain so swiftly from the skin. His own face blazed like fire from the slap of her hand across his cheek. He noticed, as he sat very still, the strange terror that hid beneath her bitter, staring eyes: it wasn't any terror of the law, the cheek of which she had symbolically in his person just so vigorously slapped; it wasn't any terror of what he or the machine he represented could do to her—what anyone or anything could do to her. . . . It was baffling; baffling as the undiscoverable source of any intense emotional reaction is baffling—something that drew its sustenance from roots imbedded not in the immediate present but in the past. . . .

"You will permit me to offer my apologies?" he said.

She returned vividly to the moment, and her colour swept back in a succession of bright waves.

"I am not usually so unmannerly," she said.

"Nor usually subjected to insult. The fault was mine."

Her laugh was quite harsh. "On the contrary, Lieutenant, I am accustomed to insult."

"Then why do you stay with Mrs. Endicott?" he said softly.

"Because there are some people, Lieutenant, who can only find their happiness in hell."

"Martyrs."

"Not martyrs, precisely."

"Just what, then, precisely?"

"It's a sharing, if you wish—sort of a sharing of torture."

Vague—vague. Lieutenant Valcour felt quite convinced that he would shortly begin to gibber, if the mysteries of hearts, of minds that he had dipped into during the past few hours, did not soon coalesce within the mould of reason. He began to envy his sterner compatriots on the force who confined their process-es to the comfortable fields of hard, cold facts—the "did you at five-forty-five this afternoon place the silver teaspoon on the pantry shelf, or did you not?" sort of facts. He conceded that their wholesome, plein-air tactics were quite right, and that his own, in spite of their usually successful results, were hopelessly wrong. They at least were never called liars, or slapped in the face, or found themselves helplessly swirling in a sea of meta-physics with a splendid chance of being thoroughly drowned. He forced himself to concentrate. What was it that slash of pale lips had been saying? A sharing of something . . . Of course, of torture.

"You mean," he said, "a sharing that is now going on?"

"Perhaps—but especially in the past. Do you believe, Lieu-tenant, that the dead remain in emotional touch with the liv-ing?"

"And that, my poor fish," he told himself severely, "is what your interminable probing into people's souls has got you into."

"I have never thought about it. But I should like to believe that it is true. I should like to believe in anything that offers corroborative proof of immortality."

"You are convinced of the finality of death?"

"It is a dread, not a conviction."

Roberts nodded her head swiftly. "And with me—with me— if I could only *know*."

"So that you would be quite certain that your sacrifice is not being made in vain." Lieutenant Valcour spoke very softly. He was approaching, he felt, no matter how grandiloquently, that goal toward which he had been aiming: the answer to the amazing look she had given him in Mrs. Endicott's room.

The mood broke. She stood up abruptly.

"You wished that address book?" she said.

It was of no great matter. Moods, at least, did not die. They were always there—somewhere—waiting to be recaptured.

"If you will be so kind," he said.

She went to the door of Mrs. Endicott's room, opened it, was swallowed up. Lieutenant Valcour waited outside. The case was becoming mired in evasions. That was the trouble with cases whose milieu rose beyond a certain social and mental level. They invariably grew kaleidoscopic with overtones. Crime in the lower strata was noteworthy for its crudenesses rather than its subtleties: an intrigue among animals, with the general patentness of some jackal filching its prey. But breeding and intellect generally presupposed masks: the inbred defensiveness of manner and social combativeness with the world which offered barriers most difficult to pierce. Roberts opened the door and handed him the small leather reference book Mrs. Endicott had used when verifying the telephone number of Dr. Worth.

"Thomas Hollander," she said. "The names are listed alphabetically."

The door closed even in that short second which preceded his thanks. It was a gesture of retreat from hinted intimacies. It wasn't so much the door of the room she had closed as it was the door guarding her secrets. He felt that she wanted to show him she had already repented of having gone so far—not that she *had* gone any distance, really, but there were beacons, faint pin points of light toward which he would chart a course over the surface of her troubled seas.

He took the reference book and sat down. He began with A and started to go systematically through it. At H he fixed in his memory the street and telephone number of Hollander's house. He continued without interest to turn the pages.

At the end of the M's he came, to his marked bewilderment, upon the address and telephone number of Marge Myles.

# CHAPTER X
## 12:06 *a. m.*—The Stillness of a Grave

Lieutenant Valcour went to the head of the stairs. "O'Brian!" he called down.

O'Brian looked up at him from below.

"Yes, Lieutenant?"

"Send Hansen up here, please."

"Yes, sir."

A painting on the wall held Lieutenant Valcour's attention while he waited. A Gauguin, he thought, and, going closer, confirmed it. His eye drifted over the entire corridor. Everywhere were the details of great wealth, and the young owner of it all not a happy child of kind fortune, but a detested, a passionately hated, and a passionately loved man. There flashed again before him in brief review Mrs. Endicott, a storehouse of mountain storms in summer; Mrs. Siddons, spiritual ash; Roberts, the shortest step this side of some fervour bred in the swamps of lunacy; Hollander—Marge Myles—who knew? And would one ever know? Suppose, as Dr. Worth had more than hinted, Endicott should refuse to speak—if that strange reticence harped upon so insistently both by his wife and his physician should resist . . .

"Lieutenant, sir, Officer Hansen reporting."

Lieutenant Valcour dragged his eyes from the Gauguin unwillingly.

"All right, Hansen," he said. "Come with me."

They went down the corridor and stopped before the door to Endicott's room.

"Do you know what's gone on here to-night, Hansen?"

"From what I've heard, sir, the man who was thought dead is now alive."

"That is correct."

Lieutenant Valcour opened the door and beckoned to Cassidy. Cassidy came out and joined them.

"When you two men go back into that room," Lieutenant Valcour said, "I want you to get a couple of chairs and sit down just inside the bathroom doorway. Put the chairs where you can watch the bed and this hall door. If you talk, use a low voice that won't disturb either the patient or the nurse, and from the moment when she indicates that he's returning to consciousness, say nothing at all and sit still. The shock of knowing that you were there might disturb his heart again. Is that clear?"

They assured him, in unison, that it was.

"This hall door," Lieutenant Valcour went on, "is going to be kept locked on the inside by the nurse. Every time she opens it, watch carefully. Keep your eye on anyone who comes into the room, especially if they offer some excuse for wanting to be there—and when I say 'anyone,' I mean just that. For instance: the nurse might want some coffee and ring for a servant. Watch that servant every second until she goes and the door is locked again. While on the subject of coffee, you will drink none that may be offered you while you're on watch."

"I never drink coffee, Lieutenant," said Cassidy. "Now if it was a cup of tea——"

"If you get thirsty," said Lieutenant Valcour severely, "take some water from the tap. And eat nothing at all. I don't want to have to come back here and find you both groggy with knock-out drops and with heaven-knows-what happened to Endicott. Mind you, I'm not suggesting that anything like this will happen—but it might. Clear?"

Again, in unison, they assured him it was all most clear.

"Keep in mind," Lieutenant Valcour went on, "that primarily you are in a sick-room over which Dr. Worth has absolute charge. You are not to interfere with anything he may do, or with any arrangements he may make during the night. You are only to step in if you see that Endicott's life is threatened through the action of some person who may approach him. Try to prevent this by physically overpowering the attacker if you can, but if there is no time for that do not hesitate to shoot."

"Even if it's a woman, Lieutenant?" said Hansen quietly.

Lieutenant Valcour shrugged. "There are no such things," he said evenly, "as sex or chivalry in murder."

"Yes, sir."

"I am painting, incidentally, the darkest prospect of the picture. In all probability nothing will happen at all. You'll spend a sleepless and tiresome night, get cricks in your necks, and damn the day you ever joined the force. Now, then, there is one thing more, and that concerns a man by the name of Thomas Hollander. Dr. Worth believes it advisable that an intimate friend of Endicott be near him and be the first person whom Endicott sees when he recovers consciousness. Mr. Hollander is that friend. I am going to try to get in touch with him shortly, explain matters to him, and get him to come up here. Mr. Hollander is naturally the exception to my previous instructions. Let him alone. Don't interfere with him, but—" Lieutenant Valcour's pause was significantly impressive "—watch him. Watch him, my good young men, as two harmonious cats might watch a promenading and near-sighted mouse. Shall I repeat?"

"I get you, Lieutenant," said Cassidy. And Hansen, he was assured, had "got" him, too.

"Then we will go in, and you will establish yourselves for the night at once."

He opened the door, and they went inside. Dr Worth's arrangements were complete, and he was ready to turn in. Nurse Murrow had received her instructions and was to call Dr. Worth should Endicott show any symptoms of returning consciousness.

Dr. Worth joined Lieutenant Valcour at the door.

"There is nothing further we can do for the present, Lieutenant, except wait," he said.

"All right, Doctor. I've told my men how things stand." He nodded toward Cassidy and Hansen, who, on tiptoe, were vanishing into the bathroom with two chairs. "I've told them you're in charge here, and that there's not to be an unnecessary sound or move out of them."

Dr. Worth continued to remain politely incredulous. "Well, I dare say you know what you are doing, but it still seems an extraordinary precaution to me."

"And it probably is. I spoke to one of the maids about your staying here, Doctor."

"Yes—thank you. They've told me where my room is. It's the one directly above this one."

"I've also lined up one of Endicott's friends. I'm getting in touch with him directly, and when he comes I'll have him sent up to you. You can tell him just what you want him to do, and then see that he gets in here all right, if you will, please."

"By all means. Who is he, Lieutenant?"

"A Mr. Thomas Hollander—lives on East Fifty-second Street."

"Never heard of him; but there's no reason why I should have." He sped a parting look toward Endicott, faintly breathing on the bed. "The most reticent man, Lieutenant, whom I have ever met."

They went outside and closed the door.

Nurse Murrow went over and locked it. She felt, to put it mildly, not a little atwitter. Her life had not conformed to the popular version of a trained nurse's. There had been no romantic patients in it whose pallid, interesting brows she had smoothly divorced from fever by a gentle pass or two with magnetic fingers. No grateful millionaire had offered her his heart and name; nor had any motherly-eyed old dowager died and willed her a fortune. No. There had been, on the other hand, a good many years of sloppy, disillusioning, grilling work, long hours spent in pampering peevish patients, patients who were ugly with that special ugliness which is inherent in the sick, snappish doctors, and a perfect desert of romance.

The present case loomed as a heaven-sent oasis. Who knew what might not develop out of it? It awakened all the atrophied hunger of her starved sentimentalism. And even if nothing *did* result from it—nothing practical, like marriage, or a good bonus—it would at least leave her something to think about during those endless, tiresome, tiring hours of the future. . . .

She crossed to the bed and looked down at Endicott. She felt his pulse and made a notation on her night chart. She lingered near the bathroom doorway.

"The strangest case," she whispered, "that I've ever been on."

Cassidy looked up at her bleakly.

Hansen said, "Yes, ma'am."

"I dare say," she whispered on, "that it's quite in the ordinary run of things for you gentlemen."

"Yes, ma'am."

"There's an atmosphere—a something sinister——"

"Yes, ma'am."

Nurse Murrow's broad shoulders jerked impatiently. There was a talk-chilling quality in being so determinedly ma'am'd. She gave it up, and settled herself starchily in an armchair. She adjusted a lamp so that it shaded more efficiently her eyes.

A floor board creaked upstairs—once.

That would be Dr. Worth, she decided, going to bed. What a man! What a shining light in his profession! A little bigoted, perhaps, in some things, but so distinguished—admirable—a bachelor, too—— But what nonsense!

A complete stillness settled gently on the house. The stillness of a grave.

Yes, she thought, just exactly that—the stillness of a grave. . . .

# CHAPTER XI
## 12:15 *a. m.*—To Watch by Night

Lieutenant Valcour refreshed his memory from the leather reference book and then dialled the number.

"Mr. Thomas Hollander?" he said, when a man's voice answered him. It was a smooth, soft voice, and he suspected that further words beyond the initial "hello" would reveal a Southern accent.

"Who is calling, please?" went on the voice, making the expected latitudinal revelation.

"I have a message from the home of Mr. Herbert Endicott for Mr. Thomas Hollander. Will you ask him to come to the 'phone, please?"

"One moment."

"Certainly."

Lieutenant Valcour drew stars on a scratch pad while he waited. He wondered idly what secret powers or hidden vices they would disclose if examined by a trained graphologist. He made quite a good star and drew exciting rays out from its points. That would undoubtedly show, he told himself, that he was a nosey, mean-spirited, and cold-hearted sleuth hound. What an infernal time it took to get Hollander to the telehone! Had the line gone dead? Ah . . .

"Yes?" It was a deeper voice, this time, and held no promise, or threat, of Southern softnesses.

"Mr. Thomas Hollander?"

"Yes."

"This is the home of Mr. Herbert Endicott, Mr. Hollander."

"Yes?"

"And I am Lieutenant Valcour talking—of the police."

The deadness of the wire became a pause of the first magnitude. Then:

"Well, Lieutenant, what's it all about?"

"It is about Mr. Endicott, Mr. Hollander."

"Yes?"

"Yes."

Another pause.

"He's dead?"

"Dead? Why no, Hollander. Were you expecting him to be?"

"What do you mean by 'expecting him to be'? Certainly I wasn't. Please come down to facts, Lieutenant."

"I was about to. Mr. Endicott has suffered a heart attack brought on by some sudden shock. His condition is serious, and Dr. Worth, who is attending him, insists that some friend be at hand when Mr. Endicott recovers consciousness."

"You mean"—the voice was speaking very carefully now—"in addition to Mrs. Endicott?"

"No, unfortunately Mrs. Endicott cannot be present."

Again a pause, and then:

"Why not, Lieutenant? She isn't—that is——"

"I beg your pardon, Mr. Hollander?"

"Damn it, is she arrested?"

"Certainly not. What for?"

"Well, what in hell are you cops in the house for if"—the voice ended less belligerently—"there hasn't been some crime?"

Lieutenant Valcour remained splendidly detached.

"We shan't be certain that there either has or hasn't been a crime, as you infer, until Mr. Endicott recovers consciousness and lets us know."

"He's unconscious?"

"Yes."

"Is his condition serious, Lieutenant?"

"Most serious, Mr. Hollander."

"And Mrs. Endicott—why is it she can't be with Herb?"

"Dr. Worth has given her a narcotic. She's sleeping. Her nerves are unstrung."

This evidently took a minute to digest.

"From what, Lieutenant?"

"From her husband's condition."

"Did Mrs. Endicott suggest that you call me up, Lieutenant?"

"No. Roberts, her maid, said you were a friend—a mutual friend. Roberts tells me that your name is the only one she has ever heard spoken by Mr. Endicott in terms that would imply intimacy."

"That's right."

"You and Mr. Endicott are intimate friends, are you not?"

"Pretty thick, Lieutenant. What is it you want me to do?"

"To sit with Mr. Endicott until he recovers consciousness. Dr. Worth is afraid that his heart will go back on him again if there isn't someone he knows with him when he comes to. If you'll be kind enough to come up, Dr. Worth will explain the whole peculiar affair to you much better than I can."

"Why, of course. Yes. When?"

"As soon as convenient."

"In about an hour? There are some things——"

"That will do perfectly. Thank you very much, Mr. Holland-er. Good-bye."

"Good-bye."

Lieutenant Valcour hung up the receiver of the hall telephone he was using and walked to where he had left his coat and hat. He put them on and buttonholed O'Brian by the front door.

"O'Brian," he said, "there's a man coming here shortly by the name of Thomas Hollander. Have him identify himself by a vis-iting card, or a letter, or his driver's licence, or initials on some-thing or other. Give him a pat, too, in passing to make certain that he hasn't got a gun. If it offends him, say that it is just a matter of routine. As a matter of fact, in his case, it probably is. Then show him up to the room that Dr. Worth is occupying for the night."

"Yes, sir."

"From Dr. Worth's room he will be taken down to Mr. End-icott's room and will stay there until morning."

"Yes, sir."

"I want you to tip the men off on guard down here that I want it known I am going home until tomorrow. Tell Mr. Hol-lander that if he asks to see me. I am leaving the house now and may be gone for a couple of hours, more or less. Then I'm com-ing back. I'll rap on this door here, and you let me in."

"Yes, sir."

"There's probably a lounge or something in that room there just off this hall. I'll spend the night on it."

"Yes, sir."

"What is the name of the gentleman who is coming?"

"Thomas Hollander, Lieutenant."

"Good."

Lieutenant Valcour went outside. The normal orderliness of life returned comfortingly with the first deep breaths of cold night air. He walked the short half block to Fifth Avenue and hailed a taxi. He got in. He gave the driver, through the half-opened window in front, the Riverside Drive address of Marge Myles.

# CHAPTER XII
## 12:30 *a. m*—Madame Velasquez Stirs up Muck

THE TAXI ran north along Fifth Avenue for a few blocks and then bore left into the leafless, frosty stretches of Central Park. It was deserted of pedestrians. Occasional yellow lights showed the vacant surface of benches and empty walks.

The average worthlessness of any person's reactions when suddenly confronted by the police, Lieutenant Valcour reflected, was a curious phenomenon. It was his belief that only rarely were such reactions the result of the moment at hand. They were instead a subconscious scurrying backward to some earlier time when something had been done by that person, or known by that person, which might then have brought him into the grip of the law. No one—he included himself in the arraignment—led a blameless life. No, not even the saints, for they had their periods of expiation, which in themselves presupposed blemishes that required the act of expiation for their erasure. And so it was with people when, even in the rôle of the most innocent of bystanders, they were confronted by the police. Inevitably there lurked a certain fear, an instinctive thrusting out of defenses as a guard against the chance discovery of that early blemish. . . .

Take Hollander, for instance. Every word of his telephone conversation had been a negative defense, and yet one could not link it necessarily with the attack on Endicott. No, not necessarily. It was perfectly obvious that Hollander had *expected* something to happen to Endicott, and equally obvious that he was worried about the fact that Mrs. Endicott might be involved in it, but one couldn't say that he had been involved in it himself. . . .

The taxi stopped. Lieutenant Valcour got out, paid the driver, and dismissed him.

Riverside Drive seemed about ten degrees colder than the midtown section of the city had been. Or was it fifteen or twenty degrees? A northerly wind blew iced blasts from the Hudson River and at him across the treetops of the terraced park. Marge Myles, Lieutenant Valcour decided as he took in the façade of the building that housed her apartment, did herself rather well.

A sleepy and irritable Negro casually asked him "Wha' floor—'n' who, suh?" as he entered the overheated lobby. The boy was smartly snapped into full consciousness by the view offered him of Lieutenant Valcour's gold badge.

The proper floor proved to be the fourteenth.

As the hour was hovering about one in the morning, Lieutenant Valcour was considerably surprised at the promptness with which the door swung open in response to his ring, and considerably more surprised by the querulous voice that emerged from beneath a wig, dimly seen in the poor light of a foyer, and said, "Well, I must say you took your own time in coming. Put your coat and hat on that table there, and then come into the parlour."

Lieutenant Valcour complied. He followed a dimmish mass

of jet bugles into the more accurate light of a room heavily cluttered with gold-leafed furniture and brocades.

"I'm Madame Velasquez—Marge's ma. I ain't Spanish myself, but if there ever was a Spaniard, my late husband Alvarez was."

The wig on Madame Velasquez's head offered no anachronism to the bugles of her low-cut dress. Its reddish russet strands were pompadoured and puffed and showed at unexpected places little sprays of determined curls. The face beneath it bore an odd resemblance to an enamelled nut to which nature, in a moment of freakish humour, had added features.

"Now I want you to tell me at once, Mr. Endicott, what you have done with my little Marge."

Lieutenant Valcour with curious eyes tried to probe a closed door at the other end of the room.

"I expected to find her here, Madame Velasquez," he said quietly. "Isn't she?"

"She ain't. And what is furthermore, Mr. Herbert Endicott, you know she ain't." Her voice had grown shrill, but without much volume. It was rather the ineffective piping of some winded bird.

"What makes you say that, Madame Velasquez?"

The bunched strands of artificial jewellery that were recklessly clasped about Madame Velasquez's thin neck quivered defiantly.

"And you never met her here at seven," she said. "I suppose you'll say you *wasn't* to meet her here at seven. Well, I got this note to prove it. There, now."

She handed Lieutenant Valcour a sheet of notepaper that reeked of some high-powered scent.

Make yourself at home, Ma [read the note]. Herb Endicott was to meet me here at seven. He didn't come although he was to take me to the Colonial for dinner. I am going to the Colonial now and see if he is there. Maybe I did not understand him right, Ma. I will be home soon anyways.

MARGE.

"And it is now," said Madame Velasquez, "after 1 A. M."

"She knew you were going to pay her this visit, Madame Velasquez?"

"I telegraphed her this afternoon. I'm here for a week. Where is she?"

"I don't know where she is, Madame Velasquez."

"Mr. Endicott, one more lie like that and I'll call the police."

"That's all right, Madame Velasquez. You see, I am the police."

The bugles, the jewels, the curls became still with shocking abruptness, as a brake that without warning binds tightly.

"You belong to the police?"

"Yes, Madame Velasquez—Lieutenant Valcour."

He showed his badge.

"Then you ain't Mr. Endicott?"

"No, Madame Velasquez."

"Then he—she—they've gone and done it, Lieutenant—they have run away." Madame Velasquez began to simper.

"I'm sorry, Madame Velasquez, but they haven't run away. Mr. Endicott, you see, was attacked this evening. If he doesn't live, whoever did it will be charged with murder."

There was a complete absence of expression in Madame Velasquez's tone. "And you think Marge done it," she said.

"Not necessarily so at all. Your daughter may very well have met somebody else at the Colonial—some other party of friends—and have joined it when Mr. Endicott failed to show up. The Colonial is closed by now, but perhaps she went on to some night club. I shouldn't worry."

"Why should she go on to some night club when she knew her ma was waiting for her here?"

Madame Velasquez's thin hands, the fingers of which were loaded with cheap rings, played nervously with any substance they chanced to touch.

"Something's happened to her, Lieutenant," she went on. "I always told her as how it would. Marge—I told her a hundred times if I ever told her once—there's a limit to the number of suckers you can play at one and the same time."

"You think that some man who was jealous perhaps attacked Endicott first and then got after her?"

"Man? Men, Lieutenant, men. That brat kept the opposite of a harem, if you know what I mean."

"She isn't your daughter, really, is she, Madame Velasquez?"

"She was Alvarez's only child by his first wife—some Spanish female hussy from Seville. What made you guess?"

"The way you talked about her. But do keep right on, Madame Velasquez. What a remarkable pendant—it's a rarity to see so perfect a ruby—may I?"

Madame Velasquez simpered audibly while Lieutenant Valcour leaned forward and stared earnestly at the bit of paste.

"My late husband, Lieutenant, used to say that nothing was too good for pretty Miramar. That's my name, Lieutenant—Miramar."

"Few people are so happily named, Madame Velasquez. Tell me—let me rely upon your woman's intuition—just what did Marge expect from Endicott?"

Madame Velasquez leaned forward confidentially. An atmosphere as of frenzied heliotropes clung thickly about her.

"Every last damn nickel she could get," she said.

"Lieutenant Valcour assumed his most winning smile. "Scarcely an *affaire du cœur*, Madame Velasquez." If he had had a moustache, he would have twirled it. "I suppose her early marriage embittered her, rather hardened her against men?"

"Well, if it did I ain't noticed it none."

"Perhaps Endicott came under the heading of business rather than pleasure?"

"Well, yes, and then no."

"A happy combination?"

"Just a combination. Not so damn happy."

"A little bickering now and then?"

"A lot."

"Indeed? Marge was on the stage, wasn't she?"

"If you can call it the stage nowadays, Lieutenant."

"In the chorus, wasn't she?"

"Yes."

"And Harry Myles saw her and carried her off."

Madame Velasquez's laugh was an art; unfortunately not a lost one. "The millionaire marriage," she gasped. "My dear"— her hand found a resting place on one of Lieutenant Valcour's knees—"he didn't have a cent."

"She felt disappointed, I suppose?"

"Disappointed!" Madame Velasquez fairly screamed the word at him, like an angry parrot. Her manner changed and became darkly mysterious. "I know my little know," she said. "You can believe me, Lieutenant, little Miramar's not the boob some parties I could mention, but won't, think she is." Her voice grew harsh with the gritty quality of a file. "I'll learn her to leave me in the ditch like this."

"Then you think Marge purposely isn't here to greet you?"

It was a sweet little bunch of filth, taken all in all, thought Lieutenant Valcour. It was perfectly plain: Madame Velasquez either held definite knowledge that Marge had killed Harry Myles, or else had convinced Marge that she knew. And then Madame Velasquez had simply bled Marge of all the money she could get.

"Is Marge frightened easily, Madame Velasquez?"

"About some things."

The reddish, dusty-looking curls nodded vigorously. Lieutenant Valcour looked at his watch. It was one-thirty. He stood up.

"Thank you for receiving me, Madame Velasquez. If I leave you a telephone number would you care to call me up when Marge comes in? Or will you be in bed?"

"Leave your number, Lieutenant." The seamy enamelled face became more nutlike than ever. "I got a thing or two to talk over with that female Brigham Young." She raised a beringed hand and held it unescapably close to Lieutenant Valcour's lips.

He brushed them gently against a hardened coat of whiting, smiled his pleasantest, and left, assisted doorward by what might at one time have been called a sigh.

He paused for a moment in the small foyer, after putting on his hat and coat, and pencilled the Endicotts' telephone number on one of his cards. He started back to give it to Madame Velasquez.

She wasn't in the room where he had left her, and the room's other door stood ajar. He crossed to it softly and looked in. Madame Velasquez—yes, he convinced himself, it *was* Madame Velasquez—was sitting before a dresser. Her wig was off, and her heavily enamelled face peered into a mirror beneath thin knots of corn-gray hair. As the lonely, weak old voice rose and fell, Lieutenant Valcour caught a word or two of what Madame Velasquez was saying:

"He didn't know—if I went and told her once, I told her a thousand times—he didn't *know.*" There followed a short, dreadful noise that passed as laughter. "But *I* know—Miramar knows, darling—you little lousy . . ."

Lieutenant Valcour retreated softly. He left the card lying on a table. He went outside and closed the door. He rang for the elevator and shut his eyes while waiting for it to come up. There were times when they grew a little weary from looking too intimately upon life.

Down in the lobby he used the house telephone and called up the Endicotts'.

"Lieutenant Valcour talking," he said.

"O'Brian, sir."

"Everything quiet?"

"Indeed and it is, sir."

"Mr. Hollander get there yet?"

"He's just this minute after arriving, sir. He's upstairs with Dr. Worth now."

"Did he identify himself all right?"

"He did that, Lieutenant, with cards and a driver's licence."

"Good. I'll be along in about an hour now. Good-bye."

He was helped by the bitter wind as he walked east to Broadway. He found a taxi and gave the driver Hollander's address on East Fifty-second Street. He settled back and closed his eyes. He went to sleep.

# CHAPTER XIII
## 2:01 *a. m.*—Glittering Eyes

NURSE MURROW didn't slumber, exactly; it was much too slender a lapse from consciousness for that. But it was not until the second gentle rapping that she stood up.

Someone was rapping on the hall door.

She glanced at her wrist watch as she crossed the room, and was glad to note that it was just after two o'clock. Three or four hours, now, and it would be dawn. She'd get some coffee, then, and her work for the night would be almost over.

As she turned the key in the lock she noticed with a sharp thrill of interest that the two policemen, very quiet, very alert, but still sitting on their chairs in the bathroom doorway, had each drawn a gun from its holster and was holding it by his side. She opened the door.

Dr. Worth, his dignity considerably muffled in camel's hair, stood in the corridor with a stranger.

"Miss Murrow," he said, "this is Mr. Thomas Hollander, the friend who is going to sit up with Mr. Endicott. He understands everything about the situation, and I have advised him just what to do."

"Yes, Doctor."

Dr. Worth failed futilely in suppressing a yawn. "Are there any reports?"

"No, Doctor."

"Then I'll return to my room. Call me at the slightest indication."

"Yes, Doctor."

Hollander came inside. Miss Murrow closed the door and locked it again. She stood watching Hollander as he went an uncertain step or two toward the bed, with that natural hesitation with which one approaches the very ill. He was a personable young man in his thirties. He was more than personable, she decided. Not handsome, exactly—heavens, no—she corrected herself rapidly. The features weren't moulded in the tiresome regularity of handsomeness. Engaging? Perhaps. A body perfectly proportioned, with the broad shoulders and slim hips of a fighter—of, yes, a prize fighter—an amateur sportsman.

Hollander had finished with staring down at Endicott. His walk, as he came over to where she was standing, caused Miss Murrow to change her opinion as to his vocation. She put him down as a sailor, a yachtsman. There was a buoyancy, a certain fluidity, in his movements, as if his feet were accustomed to maintaining him with poise across the surfaces of moving things. His eyes, except for one flashing glance, did not meet her own directly.

"Is it all right to smoke?" he said.

Miss Murrow smiled apologetically. "I'm afraid not, Mr. Hollander. Mr. Endicott's lungs require as clear air as possible. I've even opened that window a little to keep the atmosphere in the room quite fresh." She nodded toward the window above the large mahogany chest. The sash was up about six or seven inches from the bottom.

"Oh." Hollander continued to stand before her, giving her still that peculiar effect of movement. There was nothing perceptible about it. His body was like a stolid field, motionless, beneath drifting shadows of the clouds. "Will Dr. Worth be here when Herb comes to?"

Nurse Murrow felt a professional stiffening. "I will inform Dr. Worth at the first sign of returning consciousness."

"How?"

"I beg your pardon?"

"How'll you inform him?"

"By going up to his room, of course."

"Oh." Hollander's gaze wavered about at the line of her chin. "Then I'll just baby Herb along until you get back down here with the doctor."

"The doctor and I will undoubtedly be back before Mr. Endicott actually does come to."

"Uh-huh. Good kid, Herb."

She threw out a tentative feeler.

"You and he are great friends, Mr. Hollander?"

"Buddies. War buddies."

Miss Murrow's thoughts fled back along old trails. "How splendid! So few war friendships have really lasted, Mr. Hollander. I know it's been so in my case, and with so many, many others." A faint flush crept over her palish cheeks and made her look rather young again. "There was a girl with me in hospital at Chaumont, and we just knew we were going to be friends for life, but she lives out in Akron, Ohio."

"Uh-huh."

"We wrote quite regularly for a while after we got back from

France—we both sailed from Brest on the *Amerika*—but then it sort of dwindled. Postal cards—picture postal cards at Christmas. Last year we didn't even send any. I wonder what she'd be like if I saw her again. Have you ever wondered about people whom you've once been very fond of, that way—about whether they change in time, I mean?"

"Everything changes."

"Doesn't it, though? Just like the seasons. Oh, I do think you can draw so many happy comparisons between life and nature. They're interlinked, if you get what I mean. That's why the weather is so affecting. I just can't *help* feeling gloomy on a gloomy day, and when it's bright and cheerful and all sunshiny outside, why then I'm that way, too."

"Cripes!" muttered Hollander softly.

"What did you say, Mr. Hollander?"

"I said that was nice."

"Now I suppose with you and Mr. Endicott you see each other quite regularly."

"Now and then."

"I suppose whenever your business permits?"

His look flicked her like a whip.

"Where'll I sit?" he said.

Nurse Murrow vanished within her professional sphere.

"Near the patient, please."

She wondered whether he had meant to snub her. It wasn't a snub exactly. Yes, it was, too. Well, what of it? He was attractive enough to get away with it, and it probably was nothing but brusqueness, after all. Many strong men were brusque—purposely so to hide a tender interior. There was a man, and a millionaire at that . . . Hollander was back again beside her. She wondered whether it was so—whether people who didn't look into your eyes were people whom it was unsafe to trust.

"Just what do you know about all this?" he said softly.

"About all what, Mr. Hollander?"

"About the police being in the house."

"Isn't it just too thrilling?"

"Uh-huh. Whom do they suspect?"

Miss Murrow began to feel friendly again. He *was* so good-looking. She wished she had a whole lot of exciting and important information to give him that would keep him standing there listening, so that she could just stare at him and try to put her finger on the source of that amazing effect of fluidity.

"They haven't said whom they suspect, really." She lowered her voice to an appropriate pitch. "But I know they think it's somebody who is in the house."

Hollander's voice was a whisper. "You wouldn't say it was Mrs. Endicott whom they suspect, would you?"

Miss Murrow appeared a trifle shocked. "Oh, it would be too dreadful to think a wife would harm a husband. But it does happen." Her mind tabulated the news offered daily by the papers. "Why, it happens almost every day. Oh, you don't *think*——"

"Certainly I don't think she did it," Hollander said fiercely. "It's what the police think that I'm trying to get at. What makes you so sure they're going to hang it onto somebody who's in the house?"

Miss Murrow nodded toward the bathroom door. "From the way they're guarding Mr. Endicott from being attacked again. From being attacked," she added, "before he can make a statement."

"Then they're still just guessing?"

"Just guessing."

It seemed to satisfy Hollander, and he managed to convey the impression that the conversation, so far as he was concerned, had come to an end. Miss Murrow went over to her chair in a corner of the room and sat down. He was deep, she decided. Yes, a deep creature, with deep impulses. . . .

Cassidy and Hansen tilted back their chairs a bit and, with loosened collars, settled for the last tiring watches of the night. They had nodded briefly to Hollander, and he had nodded just as briefly in return. He looked to them like a good scout. Like one of the boys. Regular. Cassidy tried to remember what that last line of hooey was that the lieutenant had shot at them about Hollander. Something about cats. About two cats, that was it, watching a promenading and near-sighted mouse. Nuts.

Hollander took an armchair and pushed it close to the head of the bed. It was an upholstered armchair, heavy, and with a tall solid back. He placed it so that its back was to the bathroom door. The back also obliquely obscured him from a full view on the part of Nurse Murrow. He vanished into its overstuffed depths and settled down. His eyes travelled slowly along the spread until they came to rest with a curious fixity on the smooth, masklike face of his friend Endicott.

Then the pupils of Hollander's eyes contracted until they glittered like the heads of two bright pins.

# CHAPTER XIV
## 2:01 *a. m.*—An Empty Sheath

IT WAS just after two o'clock when Lieutenant Valcour stepped to the pavement and paid his fare to the driver. The cab snorted away and left silence hanging heavy on the street. The bachelor apartment house where Hollander lived had an English basement entrance. He found Hollander's name among a row of five others and pressed the proper button. After he had pressed it four times, a voice answered him through the earpiece of the announcer.

"Who and what is it?" said the voice.

It was the Southern voice.

"This is Lieutenant Valcour of the police department talking."

"Oh. Mr. Hollander has already left, Lieutenant."

"Thank you, I know that. I want to come upstairs."

"Fourth floor, Lieutenant—automatic lift."

"Thank you."

The release mechanism on the door was already clicking. Lieutenant Valcour entered a smart little lobby and then an electric lift. He pressed the button for the fourth floor.

"Sorry to bother you like this," he said, as he stepped out into a private foyer, and stared curiously at the young man facing him.

"No trouble at all, Lieutenant."

"That's very kind of you, Mr.——"

"Smith, Lieutenant—Jerry Smith."

"Since when?" asked Lieutenant Valcour gently, as he started to follow Mr. Smith into an adjoining room.

"Why, what do you mean, Lieutenant?"

The man stopped, and his soft dark eyes stared earnestly at Lieutenant Valcour from a ruddy, slightly dissipated-looking young face.

Lieutenant Valcour removed his hat and placed it on a settee. "Nothing much, Mr. Smith," he said. "Certainly nothing beyond the fact that I saw you one morning last month in the line-up down at headquarters. In connection with some night-club business, I believe. The charge fell through, I also believe, because the woman involved preferred the loss of her emerald necklace to the loss of prestige she certainly would have suffered during the publicity of a trial had she pressed the case. That's all I mean, Mr. Smith."

"I don't suppose, sir, I could convince you of my innocence?"

"No, I don't suppose you could."

"It was my misfortune that the case never did come to trial, Lieutenant. I could have cleared myself then."

"Nonsense. You could have brought counter charges—sued for damage for false arrest."

Mr. Smith looked inexpressibly shocked. "We of the South, sir, do not bring charges against a lady."

"Well, the ethical distinction between swiping a woman's necklace and bringing charges against her is a shade too delicate for my Northern nerves to grasp." Lieutenant Valcour crossed casually to a chair placed before a secretary and sat down. "Sit down, Mr. Smith," he said, "and tell me something about your friend Thomas."

"The straightest, squarest gentleman who ever lived, sir. Why . . ." Mr. Smith plunged into a panegyric that would have brought a blush even to the toughened cheek of a Caligula.

Lieutenant Valcour permitted him to plunge. While the flood poured into his ears, his eyes were inconspicuously busied with such papers as were on view in the secretary.

Tom, DARLING [he read on the folded half of a sheet of notepaper]:
Let's tea on Thursday at the Ritz. 4:30, as Herbert . . .

Lieutenant Valcour did not consider it essential to reach out and turn the page. His fingers absently busied themselves with the leather sheath for, presumably, a metal paper cutter or, perhaps, a stiletto.

"Yes, he is an honourable and an upright gentleman, sir, and if you think there is anything wrong with him in the Endicott business"—Mr. Smith temporarily moved north of the Mason and Dixon Line—"you're all wet."

Mr. Smith was through.

"For how long has he known Endicott, Mr. Smith?"

"As I've been telling you, Lieutenant, ever since that night he saved Endicott's life."

Lieutenant Valcour became almost embarrassing in the sudden focussing of his attention. "Would it bother you very much, Mr. Smith, to tell me of that occurrence again?"

"Why, it's just as I've been *saying*, Lieutenant, in the war—the war."

"Oh, of course. Endicott and Hollander were in the same outfit, and Hollander saved Endicott's life."

"You can prove it, sir, if you wish. Just call up the Bronx armoury and ask for the adjutant—in the morning, of course, as he wouldn't be there now. He'll make it official."

"Oh, I believe it all right, Mr. Smith. It's a very reasonable explanation of why Endicott should be so intimate with one of your friends."

"I swear you have me wrong, Lieutenant. I had no more to do with that gilt-knuckles job than—" Mr. Smith sought desperately for a convincing simile—"than a babe unborn."

"It isn't any of my business anyway, Mr. Smith, even if you had," said Lieutenant Valcour soothingly. He tapped the leather sheath he was holding against his fingers. "I suppose Hollander was even quite prominent at the wedding, when Endicott was married?"

"Prominent? He was the best man."

"Really. Well, well. Mrs. Endicott is indeed a very beautiful woman, and from all that she has told me, a much misunderstood one."

Mr. Smith poised himself delicately upon the fence and remained watchful.

"It must have been rather a problem for Hollander," Lieutenant Valcour went on reflectively, "when she told him this afternoon during their tea at the Ritz that she was faced with one of two things."

"What do you mean, Lieutenant?"

"Didn't he tell you?"

"Tell me what, Lieutenant?"

"That Mrs. Endicott told him she couldn't stand it any longer: that she either was going to kill her husband or else commit suicide."

Mr. Smith smothered a sharp intaking of breath.

"Oh, you know how women talk, Lieutenant. It's just talk."

"Then he wasn't impressed, really?"

"Why, of course not. No more so than you or I would have been."

"He got back here from the Ritz at six?"

"About."

"And stayed here until I 'phoned him?"

Mr. Smith looked a little baffled. "Well, not exactly, Lieutenant."

"Just how exactly, Mr. Smith?"

"Why, you see, he left for dinner right after he came in."

"Just after six?"

"Near six-thirty."

"And what time did he get back from dinner?"

"I wasn't here, Lieutenant. I had a date and didn't get back here myself until around midnight."

Lieutenant Valcour became very, very casual.

"Did Hollander plan to marry Mrs. Endicott after she'd got the divorce?" he said.

"Golly, no. There wasn't going to be any divorce. It was platonic—and damned if I don't believe it."

"It's quite possible."

"I have never seen her—but to hear Tom rave!"

"She is very beautiful."

"Lieutenant," Mr. Smith's exceedingly attractive dark eyes stared solemnly into Lieutenant Valcour's veiled ones, "he thinks she's a saint. I mean it."

"Dark and strange," muttered Lieutenant Valcour. "Dark and strange."

"What's dark and strange, Lieutenant?"

"The rather terrible things that sometimes happen, Mr. Smith, under the patronage of love."

"I'll be damned if you talk like a cop," said Mr. Smith, suddenly very suspicious.

"Then I'm afraid you are damned, Mr. Smith. What," Lieutenant Valcour asked suddenly, "was kept in this?"

Mr. Smith, momentarily distracted from his suspicions by the abrupt switch, stared at the leather sheath Lieutenant Valcour was holding out at him.

"Some sort of a sticker that Tom picked up on the other side," he said. "Damascus steel, he calls it. Uses it for a paper knife."

"I wonder why it isn't in its sheath," said Lieutenant Valcour mildly.

"Search me."

Lieutenant Valcour poked around among the papers.

"It isn't here in this secretary, either."

"Well, I don't know where it is, Lieutenant. It was there this afternoon."

"I don't know where it is either, Mr. Smith, but I'm going to find out."

"Go ahead."

"Where was it you saw it this afternoon? On this secretary?"

"Yes."

Lieutenant Valcour's search of the secretary was swift and thorough. The pigeonholes, the drawers yielded no stiletto of Damascus steel. Hidden in one of the drawers was a copy of the *Oxford Book of English Verse*. That interested him momentarily. He gave it sufficient attention to note that the most used portion included the Sonnets of Shakespeare. But there was no time now—no time.

"I'm going through the rooms here," he said, "and look for that stiletto."

"You'll be exceeding your authority if you do, Lieutenant."

"Have you any objections?" Lieutenant Valcour asked quietly.

Mr. Smith grew almost fervent in his protestations that he had none. Why should he? He had nothing to conceal, nor had Hollander. Of course, there were a bottle or two of gin and a quart of Scotch, but he didn't imagine the lieutenant would be interested in anything along that line. No, the lieutenant assured him, he wouldn't be. Liquor was not in his province. Then it would be all right to go ahead and search? Lieutenant Valcour wanted to know. Oh, quite.

In spite of his verbal acquiescence Mr. Smith followed Lieutenant Valcour through the two other rooms of the apartment with a gradually growing air of truculence. He stood near and a little behind him when, after the search yielded nothing, Lieutenant Valcour went to a telephone and dialled the Endicotts' number.

Lieutenant Valcour did not get the connection, because Mr. Smith drew a pliable leather-bound slug of lead from his pocket and struck Lieutenant Valcour with it on the head.

# CHAPTER XV
## 2:13 *a. m.*—The Thin Steel Blade

Miss Murrow began to feel fidgety.

Even after the many, many years she had spent in nursing she had never accustomed herself to spending a night quite comfortably in a chair. She had always had her attacks of the fidgets, and would probably continue to have them until she arrived at the port of destination for all good nurses and married one of her patients or a doctor. Of the two she really preferred a patient.

She trained a speculative eye on her present one over there on the bed. Not really speculative, as—she told herself firmly—he was already married. Although heaven knew that that never mattered. Take the case of that red-headed Gilford girl who had snapped old man Tomlinson right up from under his wife's nose—probably, at that, because of his wife's nose, which had been an unusually large one. Miss Murrow giggled. That was almost witty enough to tell to Mr. Hollander.

He must have *felt* that she was thinking about him. What a curious expression that was in his eyes. He had just turned them toward her, and they seemed to glitter. Yes, that was the word exactly—"glitter."

It was a fancy of Miss Murrow's to be meticulous in the matter of words. "Really," she thought, "I don't see why I couldn't be an author." She felt sure she had ever so much more knowledge of life than one encountered in the average run of books. Tripe. Yes, "tripe" was indeed the word. Of course, her books wouldn't be average. Now that little story of Delia Hackenpoole and the interne with those shifty eyes . . .

Eyes . . .

Yes, Mr. Hollander's eyes *were* glittering—even in that second flash she had just caught of them. But possibly he, too, had the fidgets. He'd been sitting terribly quiet for the past ten minutes or so. Not a budge out of him. A body would forget he was there, almost.

Of course he was handsome. Especially in that soft, vague light from the distant lamp which picked his pale features out obscurely. And they *were* pale, at that. Genuinely pale. She did hope he wasn't going to be ill or have a nervous breakdown and ruin this perfectly marvellous case of the dear doctor's. . . .

Mrs. Sanford Worth. What a pleasant name it would be. *Distingué.* How apt the French were! (She knew ten phrases.)

Was that right hand of Mr. Hollander's actually moving, or was it an illusion of light and shade? It seemed to be slipping slowly from the arm of the chair and would eventually end up in his lap. It was moving—it wasn't—quite creepy, really. Damn the fidgets! She shifted her centre of balance and felt temporarily relieved. Overstuffed chairs were really wretched for prolonged periods of sitting, when you came right down to it, whereas a good old-fashioned horsehair sofa, such as Aunt Helen had had at Sciota. . . .

Why, the hand was gone!

Positively gone—like a conjuring trick.

It wasn't on the arm of the chair, so it must be in Mr. Hollander's lap. Then it *had* been moving after all, and she hadn't been just imagining it. Why, it was almost *sneaky*. . . .

His profile was toward her. Not a snub nose, exactly, nor *retroussé*. You couldn't apply that term to anything about a man, and whatever else he might be, Mr. Hollander certainly was a man.

How interesting his life at sea must have been. (She had definitely ticketed him as a sailor.) Lives at sea were always interesting. All the best books were in accord with that. You never read of a Main Street on the ocean. What with the girls in every port and the fights and the smell of crisp salt air . . . What a wretched little twirp that boy had been down at the beach last summer, with his absurd remarks about the salt smell being a lot of decayed lobster pots and dead fish. Of course the air at sea was salt. Sea and salt were synonymous.

Mr. Hollander *did* have the fidgets.

She couldn't see exactly, because of the masking arm of the chair, but he certainly was fiddling with something. She'd think he was twirling his thumbs, if he looked like the sort of man who twirled thumbs, but he didn't, so it wasn't that.

She looked at her wrist watch and saw that the hands were approaching the half hour. She'd have to examine her patient and note his pulse on the chart. What a pity that the only time you really felt comfortable in an overstuffed chair was at the moment when you had to get up.

She stood up, smoothed starched surfaces, and sailed, a smart white pinnace, toward the bed. She smiled engagingly at Mr. Hollander and then started to take Endicott's pulse. She gave a slight start and concentrated her full attention upon Endicott.

"I think there's a change."

Hollander looked up at her alertly. "Change?"

"I think he shows signs of coming to."

Miss Murrow wondered a moment at the tight little lines which suddenly appeared on Hollander's face, hardening and aging it rather shockingly, and altering the features into a cast whose hidden significance she could not define exactly. Strain, perhaps, better than anything else, served as an explanation: an emotional strain.

"How can you tell?" he said.

Miss Murrow smiled a bit superiorly. "It becomes instinct, mostly."

"Will it be soon?"

"Very soon now. Be careful, please, not to disturb him or make any sudden noise or movement until I come back. I want Dr. Worth to be on hand before the patient actually does regain consciousness."

"You going up to get him now?"

"Yes." She went over to the bathroom door and spoke to Cassidy. "You gentlemen will be careful, won't you, about being seen? I'd stay well back within the doorway, as sometimes a patient is a little, well, wild when he comes to like this, and if he started jerking around at all he might see you." She smiled engagingly. "What with the uniforms and everything——"

Miss Murrow left implications of the possible fatal consequences hanging in air and returned to Endicott. She examined him critically for another moment, checked his pulse again, and then started for the door. She stopped just before she reached it, and said to Hollander: "I suppose you had better lock the door after me. Lieutenant Valcour placed great stress on the fact that it should be kept locked constantly."

"I'll lock it," said Hollander.

"It does seem kind of foolish, doesn't it?"

Hollander smiled grimly. "Most foolish."

He stood up and joined her at the door. She went outside. He closed the door and locked it. He stared almost blankly for an instant at the two policemen. They had drawn their chairs back a little within the bathroom doorway. Hansen was impassively studying the ceiling above his head. Cassidy, leaning forward a little, was looking with solemn eyes at the outline of Endicott's still figure beneath the bedclothes.

Hollander stretched cramped muscles and then went back to his armchair beside the bed. He sat down and was all but completely obscured from the two guards by its high back. With imperceptible movements he drew a thin steel blade from beneath the cuff of his left coat sleeve and held it in such a fashion that it was masked in the palm of his right hand, the hilt extending up a little beneath the shirt cuff. He leaned forward and stared down upon Endicott's quiet face. Not quiet, exactly, for the lids were twitching—opening—and Endicott's eyes, bright and unseeing from fever, stared up. . . .

# CHAPTER XVI
## 2:13 *a. m.*—Time *versus* Death

O'BRIAN STIRRED a bit restlessly in his chair by the hall door and yawned; then he looked at his watch. It was almost a quarter past two. He began to enumerate the various things he would give for a good cup of strong black coffee, and his shirt headed the list. Or, if not coffee, some excitement to keep him awake.

The telephone jangled.

He stood up abruptly and went to the instrument. It would be, he imagined, Lieutenant Valcour calling again to find out if everything was all right. Well, everything was.

O'Brian lifted the receiver and said, "Hello!"

No one answered him, and there wasn't any sound from the other end of the line, unless you could call a sort of thumping noise and a faint tinkle that might have been breaking glass a sound.

"Hello!" O'Brian said again.

The line wasn't dead, because there wasn't that peculiar burring one hears when the connection is broken. The receiver of the 'phone at the other end was certainly off the hook. O'Brian singled out one of the patron saints of Ireland and wanted to know, most emphatically, just what sort of fun and foustie was being made of him.

"Hello!" He tried it again.

There was a click. The burring sound started. The line was dead. Whoever had been calling from the other end had hung up.

O'Brian very thoughtfully did likewise.

Then he began to wonder what he ought to do. It didn't take him very long to decide, especially as the thumping noise and tinkle of breaking glass grew louder in retrospect the more he thought about them. He didn't have to go as far as Denmark; something was certainly rotten right here in New York.

He dialled the operator, identified himself as a member of the police force, and stated that he wanted the call he had just received instantly traced.

"Oneminuteplease," requested a voice with a macadamized smile.

The minute stretched into two—ten—but eventually he was informed that the call had come from the apartment of a Mr. Thomas Hollander, whose 'phone number and address were thereupon given.

O'Brian jotted them down. He then dialled the telephone number of Hollander who was, as he very well knew, right upstairs. Several persistent diallings failed to awaken any response.

The complexion of the work afoot grew dirtier. O'Brian felt certain that it was connected with the terrain activities of Lieutenant Valcour. If it had just been some occupant of Hollander's apartment who had wanted to call Hollander up about something, there would have been an answer.

And there wouldn't have been that thumping noise, and the tinkle of breaking glass.

It seemed a matter that required investigation at once. O'Brian telephoned his precinct station and reported the occurrence and his beliefs about it to the sergeant in charge. He was assured that a raiding squad would be dispatched within a matter of minutes to the address he had given.

One was.

They found Lieutenant Valcour helplessly bound, very dazed, very weak, lying on the floor beneath a table when the men crashed the door to Hollander's apartment and broke in. Cold water—a glass of whiskey from a convenient decanter—and intelligence and strength began to return. Lieutenant Valcour pushed away the hands that were supporting him and, going to the telephone, called the Endicotts'.

"O'Brian?"

"Yes, Lieutenant—you all right, sir?"

"Yes, yes—pay attention to every word I say and follow my instructions to a letter. Endicott's life depends upon it."

"Yes, sir."

"Go upstairs to Dr. Worth and wake him. Tell him I believe that Hollander is armed with a knife and that he is probably just waiting for a chance to use it when he won't be observed by the nurse or Cassidy and Hansen. Hollander is Endicott's enemy, not friend. Tell Dr. Worth to go down and knock on Endicott's door. Tell him to go right inside when it opens. Now get this."

"Yes, sir."

"Tell him to ask the nurse how the patient is—to act natural about it. Tell him to start to go out and then, as a second thought, tell him to beckon to Hollander as if he wanted to tell Hollander something. Hollander will get up and go to him. Tell him to whisper to Hollander that there's something he wants to tell him privately, if Hollander will step outside for a minute into the corridor. You be in the corridor. When Hollander comes out, jump him. Put the cuffs on him and keep him quiet until I get there. I'll be right on up. O. K.?"

"Yes, sir."

Lieutenant Valcour rang off. He turned to the sergeant in charge of the detail.

"Leave one man here, Sergeant," he said. "The rest of you men can go back to the station after you've dropped me at the Endicotts'."

"Anything you want the man who's left here to do, Lieutenant?"

"Not unless a dark-haired youngster comes back, which he won't. But if he should, just have him kept for me, please, on ice."

Down on the street, Lieutenant Valcour jumped in beside the driver of the department car and said, "Step on it, Clancy. It's only eleven blocks up and three west."

The car shot forward, swept to the right at the corner, and lunged up Lexington Avenue. There was little traffic, and what little there was was so scattered that nothing impeded its way.

"Something going to break on that Endicott business, Lieutenant?"

"Either going to, or has."

"A homicide, ain't it?"

"Possibly—by now."

Nurse Murrow smoothed the last wrinkles from her uniform while waiting for Dr. Worth to open the door. It paid to look one's best. Always, at any time at all. One never could tell.

"Oh, Doctor. I'm sorry to get you up again so soon, but Mr. Endicott shows symptoms of coming to."

Dr. Worth, who was no longer the eager-eyed practitioner

he once had been, did his best to shake off the puffy chains of sleep.

"I'll come right down, Miss Murrow."

"I'll wait, Doctor."

"Just want to dash some cold water on my face."

"No hurry, Doctor."

He vanished into the room again. Ah, dreamed Miss Murrow, *what* a man! And he'd never been snappy with her, either. So many were snappy. Someone was coming up the stairs— quickly—two at a time—a policeman——

"Where's the doctor, miss?" said O'Brian, a little winded.

"He's coming right out, Officer."

"I gotta see him at once."

O'Brian brushed her aside and opened the door. Dr. Worth met him, astonished and glistening, on the threshold.

"Say, lissen, Doctor, the lieutenant just called up, and he said . . ."

O'Brian thereupon repeated all that the lieutenant had said.

"But, my dear man, this is the most extraordinary thing I have ever heard in my life!" Dr. Worth's slightly damp eyebrows indulged in a series of gyrations.

"Sure there ain't no time for astonishments, Doctor," said O'Brian. "Let's go—easy and quietlike, now. We're not to put this bird wise. . . ."

With O'Brian leading, they started down the stairs.

"Hello, Herb," Hollander said softly.

Endicott's voice was so weak that it scarcely carried to Hollander's ears. "Who is it?" he said. "What . . ." the voice dribbled off.

"It's your friend, Herb."

Sullen, petulant lines clung suddenly to Endicott's mouth, making the thickish lips look almost viciously weak. He made a curious noise that might have been intended for a laugh.

"Have no friend." The voice was the ghost of dead whispers.

"What happened to you, Herb?"

"Happened?" Endicott's eyes made a strong effort to get through the fogs shrouding them. "Something did happen—I want the police—I'll teach that rotten—that——"

There wasn't any sound for a while.

"You'll teach whom, Herb?"

Endicott was staring very fixedly up at Hollander now. And Hollander's right hand, the fingers of which were unnaturally rigid, was gently moving to that spot on the spread which would lie above Endicott's heart.

"Who is it you're going to teach, Herb?" Hollander said again.

The mists were clearing, and Endicott could see things almost plainly. He fixed Hollander's face into definite focus. "God damn you," he said, "for a——"

"Now, now, Herb, that isn't nice, and you don't know what you're saying."

Hollander's right hand had found the spot. It hung above it, motionless, very rigid, and the fingers very stiff.

"I'm going to call a policeman and——"

Endicott's voice was so weak as to be almost inaudible. His lips seemed as motionless as the rest of his body, which was completely inert.

"No, you're not, Herb," whispered Hollander. "And you're not going to tell, either."

Endicott got tired of looking up at Hollander. His eyes travelled fretfully along Hollander's right arm.

"Neither you nor all the devils in hell," he whispered faintly, "can stop me from telling."

And then he saw the knife.

"Can't I, Herb?"

It was the slenderest knife Endicott had ever seen. He wondered where on earth Hollander had got it. No hilt—or perhaps the hilt was cupped in Hollander's hand. A stiletto, that's what it was, and its point was pressing through the white spread at a point that lay just above his heart. Why, if the pressure kept on, it would go right into his heart. . . .

*Crack* . . .

*Crack* . . . *crack crack* . . . *crack* . . . *crack* . . .

A bullet from Cassidy's gun shattered Hollander's right wrist. Hansen's shot caught him in the right shoulder. Two bullets out of the fusillade that followed lodged, one in his right hip, and the other one farther down in the leg. Both officers, in spite of Nurse Murrow's orders, had moved into the room and were crouched on the floor where they would still be concealed from Endicott's line of vision, but where they could better and more closely observe what had been the faintly suspicious movements on the part of Hollander.

They were within four or five feet of him and still crouched below him as blood stained the white spread in a sickish smear when Hollander dragged his mangled wrist across it to the floor.

# CHAPTER XVII
## 2:40 *a. m.* —The Angle of Death's Path

THE POUNDING on the door became hysterical, and Cassidy, who for two cents would have become hysterical himself, went over and unlocked it. He found Dr. Worth, backed by scandalously excited servants and flanked by Nurse Murrow and O'Brian, pressing across the sill.

"Is it Endicott?" Dr. Worth demanded breathlessly.

"No, sir—it's Hollander. We shot the knife from his hand before he could stick it into Endicott, and then we shot him down."

"Close this door, Officer, and keep these people out. Come in with me, Miss Murrow."

Dr. Worth came into the room with Nurse Murrow. Cassidy closed the door, and the shrill clatter of excited whisperings ebbed like a tide.

"Thank God, Officer, you saved Endicott. What a mess." Dr. Worth glanced critically at Hollander, huddled on the floor by the bed in a blood-soaked heap. "You two men help Nurse Murrow. Stretch him out on that chest over there by the window. Do what you can for him, Miss Murrow, until I've taken care of Endicott."

Cassidy and Hansen lifted Hollander and carried him to the improvised cot Miss Murrow arranged with blankets and a pillow on top of the mahogany chest by the window.

Nurse Murrow then became the acme, the pink of proficiency. She dressed and bound Hollander's wounds, and applied the proper tourniquet above his shattered wrist. In her opinion, his condition was not fatally serious, when one considered his obvious physique and his probably excellent constitution—of iron—and, yes, he *was* distinctly handsome. What a pity they'd arrest him. Or perhaps he was under arrest already, although she usually associated handcuffings with arrests. But there surely wouldn't be any handcuffs now. In spite of her long familiarity with dreadful injuries she shuddered a little at that shattered wrist. And they couldn't be so soulless as to move him to prison. Dr. Worth would never permit any patient of his to be treated like that. And, after all, Hollander *was* the doctor's patient. . . .

Dr. Worth himself was standing beside her. There was a bewildered, curiously grave look on his face. She sensed intuitively what had happened.

"Mr. Endicott, Doctor?"

Dr. Worth shrugged helplessly. "He's dead."

"But I swear that knife never went in, sir," Cassidy said. "Hansen, here, and me was watching Hollander like cats. Sure we saw the knife even before it touched the bedclothes."

"Didn't Hollander have a gun, too?"

"No, sir. Why do you ask?"

"Because Endicott was killed by a bullet."

Hansen's Nordic young face grew very red and then very white. Cassidy showed nothing of what he was thinking—certainly nothing of the sickening, puzzled worry that clamped his chest—except that there was a tight clenching of his hands.

"Too bad," Cassidy said.

"Yes," agreed Dr. Worth, "it is too bad."

"You're sure, sir?"

Dr. Worth grew icily formal. "Quite," he said. He was also getting good and mad. This was the sort of thing, he told himself angrily, that taxpayers shelled out their money for. Protection! It was enough to make anybody laugh. A lot of protection the police force of New York City had been for Endicott. They'd shot him—that's what.

"But I don't see how——"

"Officer, there is no mistaking the difference between a bullet wound and one made by a knife. In this case especially it is perfectly obvious. I dare say the charge against you two men will be just technical—accidental homicide in line of duty!"

Dr. Worth did permit himself one short laugh.

"I guess so, Doctor," Cassidy said.

"And is there anything that has to be done, Officer?"

"In what way, sir?"

"Why, a report made to the medical examiner?" Dr. Worth became almost airy in his mounting anger. "This sort of starts the whole thing over again, doesn't it? I mean, won't the medical examiner have to come back up and investigate before we can move the body and—oh, well, you know the line."

"Maybe so, sir." Cassidy's face was the colour of a red tile brick, "Cripes, but I wish the lieutenant was here."

"I understand that he will be here any minute."

"You've heard from him, sir?"

Dr. Worth felt that if he didn't apply the brakes he would become positively light-headed. "Oh, yes, yes, indeed, Officer. He called up to warn me that my patient was going to be murdered and suggested that I run downstairs and stop it. Murder? Fiddlesticks—it's beginning to graduate into a catastrophe."

"What has happened here?"

Lieutenant Valcour, very pale, still very weak, and with an improvised bandage around his head, had come unobserved into the room.

"You can see," Dr. Worth said with almost insulting distinctness, "for yourself."

Dr. Worth then went on to expand. He related in detail his version of the battle—he insisted that it was a battle—which had just taken place.

Entirely apart from the natural discomfiture of his head, Lieutenant Valcour was feeling desperately glum. Under no light, no matter how favourable, could his handling of the case be considered a success. He had to his credit one slap on the face, a good crack on the head from a lead slug, and now it seemed that the very man whom they had been ordered to guard had been shot and killed by his own men. That, at least, was the impression the angry bee talking to him was obviously trying to give. Oh, it would be a *cause célèbre* all right, but he shuddered to think of just what it would be celebrated for.

"This," he said, "is nonsense."

Dr. Worth was by now thoroughly acid.

"I am glad that you are able to find in the miserable situation some element of humour, Lieutenant."

"Humour? Not humour, Doctor. I am just trying to say that the probability of Endicott's having been shot by one of my men is nonsense."

"Would it convince you, sir, were I to remove the bullet and let it speak for itself? Imperfections in the barrel leave their markings, don't they? You can then doubtless determine which one of these two young men fired the unhappy shot."

"Please don't get irritated, Doctor. I'm not trying to annoy you or to be funny. It's simply that I cannot see—just where is the wound located, Doctor?"

"In the chest."

"Cassidy, where were you and Hansen standing?"

"We was crouched on the floor just inside the room, sir—not over five feet off from Hollander," Cassidy said.

"Then consider your angles, Doctor. There's Endicott—there's about where my men were crouched. It would take pretty wild shooting for either of them to hit Endicott in the chest. In fact, one might almost consider it impossible."

Dr. Worth still hovered around zero. "From the number of innocent bystanders whom one reads about in the newspapers as having been shot down by the police——"

"That is an unfair comparison, Doctor. Those cases you refer to have all involved a chase of some sort—rapid motion—streets cluttered up with people. There was nothing like that here. I'm going to call up Central Office and ask permission for you to remove the bullet and determine the angle of its path."

"Permission, sir? And do you think it is my business or my pleasure to go probing about for bullets and determining the angles of their paths? I happen to be a specialist, sir——"

"Yes, yes, Doctor. But right now it is your business to do just that. We must have the information immediately."

"And why so, sir?"

"Because if the calibre of the bullet that killed Endicott differs from the ones in the guns of my men, or if the angle of its course proves conclusively that it could not have been fired by one of them, then the murderer is still loose about the house. He couldn't have escaped, you see, as the guards are still on duty down below."

. . . Then the murderer is still loose about the house . . .

The chilling possibilities of the statement served a good deal to cool Dr. Worth's steaming indignation. He was getting tired with being angry, anyway.

"I'm sorry I have been impatient, Lieutenant. You may be quite right, and I'll be glad to help you in any way that I can."

"Thank you, Doctor. I'll telephone Central Office from downstairs, as I want to instruct the men on guard down there to be doubly careful. If you'd care to start in probing it will be quite all right. I'll explain everything to the medical examiner. It's something, you see, that we must know. Cassidy, you and Hansen are not to leave this room. Search both it and Hollander for a gun."

"Yes, sir."

Lieutenant Valcour went out, and Dr. Worth proceeded, with the aid of Nurse Murrow, to probe.

The room had an air about it of a shambles. Cassidy and Hansen, having searched for a gun and found none, leaned dispiritedly against the wall near the chest on which Hollander was lying. They felt a measured sense of relief—had felt it, in fact, from the moment when Lieutenant Valcour had come into the room. Each knew he could never have fired that shot which had killed Endicott. And each was reasonably certain that the other couldn't have, either.

They could determine nothing from Dr. Worth's face as to how the examination was going. Neither of them looked very closely at what he was doing. Their wonderings ran along parallel lines: Hollander couldn't have had a gun or they'd have seen it or found it during their recent search. None of their shots could have gone so hopelessly wild as to have hit Endicott. But somebody did have a gun, and Endicott had been shot by it. But there had been nobody in the room with Endicott except themselves and Hollander. And Hollander couldn't have had a gun, or they'd have seen it . . . the perfect loop continued on and on. Each made the circle in his thoughts and then started in all over again. If Lieutenant Valcour hadn't reëntered the room, and if Dr. Worth hadn't just then extracted the bullet, they probably would have gone mildly mad.

"Everything's all right, Doctor," Lieutenant Valcour said. "The medical examiner was only too pleased at your kindness in helping him out. He won't be up again to-night unless I send for him. He asked me to thank you."

"Not at all, Lieutenant." Dr. Worth showed considerable excitement. "You know, it's surprising. I don't know much about the calibre of bullets, but I think you're right about the angle. Here's the bullet."

Lieutenant Valcour inspected a leaden pellet curiously and then slipped it into a pocket.

"It isn't from one of our guns, Doctor," he said.

"I'm not surprised, Lieutenant—not surprised at all. Because the angle it entered at—why, damn it, Lieutenant, it must have been fired from some place over there."

Dr. Worth indicated a problematic area which included the corner where Hollander was stretched out. Lieutenant Valcour looked just above Hollander at the window. It was the window which had been opened about six or seven inches from the bottom by Nurse Murrow so that the air for her patient would be quite fresh and clear.

It was still open.

And outside of it, as Lieutenant Valcour very well knew, ran the shallow balcony which offered not only adornment to the rear of the house but a passageway to—and from—the windows of Mrs. Endicott's room.

But Mrs. Endicott was under the influence of a narcotic, and a nurse and a maid were both in the room with her.

But were they? . . .

# CHAPTER XVIII
## 3:00 *a. m.*—Thin Haze of Dread

DR. WORTH, too, was staring at the black, impenetrable rectangle left by the opened window. It was a passageway for air, but infinitely more so was it a passageway leading to obscure recesses of the night: recesses that seemed to offer a maleficent sanctuary to hell-born secrets of distorted souls.

Who had crept along that balcony and fired that shot?

The apparent improbability of anyone from Mrs. Endicott's room having done so transplanted the problem from clear fields of logic and of simple facts into vague regions of absurd conjecturings which stared wanly out at Lieutenant Valcour through baffling curtains of darkness and of fog.

He felt a definite sense of uncertainty, and—as one does when confronted by a suggestion of the unknown—an impalpable dread. It was nothing that he could put his finger on; it seemed, absurdly, some emanation from the outer night creeping in through that rectangle of black to hang in thin hazes about the room.

"What would you suggest doing with Hollander, Doctor?" he said.

Dr. Worth, whose own thoughts had been warily browsing in disagreeable pastures, sought relief in professional preciseness.

"He would be better off in a hospital, Lieutenant. I consider his constitution to be more than sufficiently strong to obviate any danger in moving him. Are you going to arrest him?"

Lieutenant Valcour smiled faintly. "He is under arrest now, Doctor. I should like to get a few things straightened out, though, before booking him on any definite charge. Would it hurt him very much to talk with me before he is taken to the hospital?"

"Not if it weren't for too long."

"Could you give him something to revive him—to brace him up?"

"Certainly."

"Then I will have a man send for an ambulance, and I'll just talk with Hollander until it gets here."

"That will be all right."

"And if you don't mind, Doctor, I should like to be alone with him. Just he and I and—Endicott."

Dr. Worth was already busied with restoratives. "Certainly," he said. "Miss Murrow and I will be outside, if you want to call us."

"Cassidy," Lieutenant Valcour said, "wait outside in the hall, and you, Hansen, go downstairs and telephone for an ambulance. Let me know as soon as it gets here."

And in a moment Lieutenant Valcour found himself alone in the room with Endicott, with Hollander, and with those curious mists that hinted at unnamed dreads.

The restoratives were effective, and Hollander opened his eyes upon a stranger who was sitting on a chair beside the mahogany chest. He wondered idly who the stranger was. The drug which Dr. Worth had given him made him feel rather alert and smart. Any sense of pain was completely deadened. His eyes travelled leisurely about the room and hesitated at a sheet-covered object on the bed. That would be his friend called Endicott. His lids closed sharply as a reaction to some wound that was not physical.

Lieutenant Valcour stared thoughtfully down at Hollander's pale face.

"What did you do with Endicott's hat?" he said.

Hollander opened his eyes again in bewilderment. "I don't know what you're talking about," he said. "And who are you, anyhow?"

"I'm Lieutenant Valcour, Mr. Hollander. We've talked together over the telephone. The hat I'm referring to is the one that Endicott must have been wearing, or carrying in his hand, or that was some place near him when you attacked him shortly after seven this evening."

"I didn't attack him, Lieutenant." Hollander's lips were peaked-looking and didn't move very much when he talked. "I wasn't in this house until a little after one-thirty this morning—after you had called me up."

"Which did you think Mrs. Endicott would really do, Mr. Hollander?"

Hollander tried painfully to concentrate. He felt the need of being very careful of his footing: they were on dangerous ground.

"Do?"

"Yes—when she told you during tea at the Ritz that she had about reached the end and was either going to kill Mr. Endicott or commit suicide. Or didn't you really believe either?"

It seemed impossible that Hollander's face could grow any paler.

"You're crazy, Lieutenant."

"All sorts of people tell me so lots of times, Mr. Hollander. Did you have to wear Endicott's hat when you went out because you had lost your own?"

Hollander sighed fretfully. "You must think I'm awfully dumb," he said.

"Oh, not at all—well, in a few things, yes. Your choice of friends, for example. And I don't mean the Endicotts."

"Whom do you mean, Lieutenant?"

"That dark-eyed child, for one—Mr. Smith. But perhaps you don't know that his name is not Smith. I imagine that when you left him in the apartment he was still either Jack Perry or Larry Nevins. He shows great versatility, really, in his adoption of names. I was just a little surprised and disappointed at his present selection of Smith."

"You've been to my apartment, Lieutenant?"

"Yes. I had quite an enlightening talk with the present Mr. Smith. Where did you leave Endicott's hat?"

Hollander, after one peevish glare, shut his eyes.

"I can tell you pretty well what happened, you see, except for that," Lieutenant Valcour went on. "You *did* believe Mrs. Endicott this afternoon when she told you her intention. That much is fact. And now for a little fiction: either at the Ritz, or just as you were handing her into her car, you stole her purse."

Hollander's eyes snapped open and glared viciously.

"Because," Lieutenant Valcour continued, "you wanted her keys—the keys to this house. You were a little hazy as to just what it was you intended to do, but you did know that you were going to kill Endicott, and that you were going to do it before his wife either committed suicide or killed him herself. You went to your apartment and got the stiletto. Then you came back here, let yourself in with Mrs. Endicott's keys, came up to this floor and into this room. You may have been in several of the other rooms first: I don't know. Nor do I know just what you were searching for while you waited in here, either. Mrs. Endicott herself will tell me all about that later. At any rate, you were going through Endicott's clothes in that cupboard when you heard him coming. You closed the cupboard door. You were naturally nervous and upset—everyone is when contemplating or committing a crime. You were afraid there would be some slip, so you disguised yourself with dust smeared on your face. Then, either because you made some noise or else because he wanted to get something Endicott opened the cupboard door and saw you. You must have had the stiletto all ready in your hand and have looked pretty horrible altogether, because the shock of seeing you stopped his heart and he crumpled to the floor."

Hollander's eyes began to look feverish.

"His falling like that startled you," went on Lieutenant Valcour. "You felt his heart, and in pulling open his overcoat so that you could get your hand inside you ripped off the top button. What did you do with it?"

Hollander grinned faintly. "Swallowed it," he said.

Lieutenant Valcour flushed a little. "You probably put it in your pocket. You were satisfied that Endicott was dead—miraculously dead—and that you hadn't had to stab him. But he *was* dead, and you experienced the natural panic of all murderers. I don't mean that you went wild, or anything. But your mind didn't function correctly. You may have been quite calm, but it wasn't a calmness based on intelligence. You dragged Endicott into the cupboard and closed the door. You washed the dirt from your hands and face in the bathroom, combed and brushed your hair, wiped the silver clean, and then printed that curious note which Mrs. Endicott found, and which contained no significance other than to direct suspicion to some outside agency in order to shield her from becoming a suspect herself. But why did you take Endicott's hat, and where did you put it?"

"You're talking bunk, Lieutenant."

"On the contrary, Mr. Hollander, those were the moves which were made here to-night—whether you were the person who made them or not."

"Yes?"

"Yes. And it is quite within the range of possibility that if you didn't make them, then Mrs. Endicott did."

Hollander looked very worried, very tired.

"You're bluffing, Lieutenant," he said.

"And you're a very frightened man, Mr. Hollander."

"Are you going to arrest Mrs. Endicott?"

"That depends."

"Because she didn't do it."

"Why didn't she, Mr. Hollander?"

"Because she loved her husband."

"I wish you would explain to me how it is that she loved him so much that she wanted either to commit suicide or else kill him."

"Pride, Lieutenant."

Lieutenant Valcour tested the possibility of that angle. It could not, he felt, be ignored. As many outrages were yearly committed under the goadings of pride as there were committed because of jealousy and hate.

"You believe, Mr. Hollander, that the other women whom her husband played around with hurt her pride so keenly that her love became coloured with hate?"

"Why not?" A certain fierceness crept into Hollander's voice. His eyes were shining very brightly. "People don't know her as I know her. *Nobody* knows her the way I know her."

Lieutenant Valcour shrugged. "She made you hate your friend—a man you'd been through the war with—whose life you had saved."

"That's the bunk, Lieutenant."

"But you did, didn't you?"

"Oh, sure, it's all true enough, about it happening—but that stuff doesn't last."

"Friendship?"

"Among men? Hell, no." Hollander jerked his head fretfully. "Gratitude gets damned tiresome, Lieutenant, not only to give it but to get it."

"Especially," Lieutenant Valcour said gently, "if a woman comes between."

"No—no—no."

There was a complete and very convincing finality in the three negations.

"But you do love Mrs. Endicott."

"I worship her."

"And she?"

"I don't know." There was nothing obscure in Hollander's expression now, and his eyes were frankly, genuinely sincere. "Why should she? I'm nothing. Herbert was everything."

Lieutenant Valcour almost regretted having to do so when he said, "Then why, Mr. Hollander, does she address you in her notes as 'Tom, darling'?"

Hollander didn't answer for a minute. He considered the question quite seriously. "I guess it's just because she's sorry for me," he said.

"And I, personally, think that that's a pretty bum guess."

"No—listen here, Lieutenant . . ."

Hollander's voice began to wander. His sentences became broken—meaningless. It was with a sense of relief that Lieutenant Valcour saw the door open and two stretcher carriers come in followed by Dr. Worth and the ambulance surgeon. Hollander, as they carried him out, was unconscious again.

Lieutenant Valcour detained Dr. Worth at the door.

"There is something I should like to ask you," he said.

# CHAPTER XIX
## 3:15 *a. m.*—The Properties of Horror

"Doctor," Lieutenant Valcour said, "our immediate concern is to find out who fired that shot. The principal reason is quite academic: we want to catch and arrest the person who did it. A secondary reason is that many people who reach the state of mental unbalance where they are impelled to commit murder don't stop with the crime. They've tasted blood. They are in a state of abnormal acuteness, and are driven by a new fear: that of discovery and capture. To prevent being captured, they reason, why not kill again? There is nothing to be lost. You see, they can only be electrocuted once. I am presupposing, of course, that the criminal is an outsider—some person at present hidden in the house, who will make some desperate effort at escape. It is a supposition that must be entertained, even though it is not a very good one. I believe that the facts will eventually prove the criminal to be a legitimate inmate."

"That narrows the field, doesn't it, Lieutenant, to whoever was in Mrs. Endicott's room?"

"It does, unless somebody dropped a rope ladder from an upstairs window and got onto the balcony in that way. But I don't put much stock in those tricks, Doctor, any more than I do in sliding panels and trapdoors. Outside of the badger game I've never come across a sliding panel in my life, and I don't ever expect to, either."

Dr. Worth was inclined to take the idea more seriously. "But a rope ladder—there might very well be one around the house for an emergency fire escape."

"All right, who was in the room just above this one? You. Did you come down a rope ladder and shoot Endicott?"

"God's truth—my dear man——"

"Oh, be sensible, Doctor, of course you didn't. And who had the room across the hall from you, which also is above the balcony? Mrs. Siddons, the housekeeper. If you saw her, you'd scarcely picture her as hurrying up and down a rope ladder. No, Doctor, whoever was on that balcony came from Mrs. Endicott's room. We're back to the same three people: Mrs. Endicott, her maid, and her nurse."

"But Mrs. Endicott is out of the question, Lieutenant. She is still under the influence of the narcotic I gave her."

"How about the nurse, Doctor? Have you known her long?"

"Known her? Only for the several cases she has worked on with me. But she comes from the most reputable agency in the city. How about the maid?"

"I don't know."

"She is just as good a candidate for suspicion as Miss Vickers, isn't she? Why under the sun should Miss Vickers want to shoot Endicott?"

"I'm not seriously considering Miss Vickers at all. It's perfectly obvious that whoever did shoot Endicott was either directly responsible for the earlier attack during the evening or else involved in it as an accomplice."

"That might still include the maid."

"It certainly might. I wonder if you'd mind asking Miss Vickers to come in here. I'd like to question her first."

Dr. Worth nodded toward Endicott's body, covered with a sheet on the bed. "Miss Vickers, Lieutenant, being a nurse is naturally accustomed to seeing the dead, but it will be rather gruesome for the maid if you question her in here, too."

"Very gruesome, Doctor."

"Well, you know best. You're liable to have a fine case of hysterics on your hands."

"I'll risk it."

Dr. Worth left and closed the door. There again swept over Lieutenant Valcour, with the solitude, that indefinable feeling of some lurking dread. There were voices crying out to him from the subconscious, warning him of dangers that were very real, very close at hand—but the messages were indecisive, as are all instinctive things which fall beyond the charted seas of any human knowledge.

Nurse Vickers came in without the formality of knocking. Her glance toward the bed was professional and not coloured by any sign of nervousness.

"Thank you for coming, Miss Vickers. I'll only bother you for a minute."

"No bother at all, Lieutenant."

"There is just one thing I want to know: who was in the room with you and your patient at the time of the shooting?"

"Why, I couldn't say, Lieutenant, exactly."

"Why not, Miss Vickers?"

"Because I wasn't there myself. I was down in the kitchen making some coffee. I left Roberts with Mrs. Endicott. You see, there wasn't anything that had to be done except just to be there. I'm sure it was quite all right."

"Of course it was. I'm not suggesting for a minute, Miss Vickers, that I thought otherwise." Lieutenant Valcour studied the woman for a second and then said, "I just wanted to know if you could help me check up on the number of shots that were fired."

"I didn't hear any shots at all, Lieutenant, 'way down there in that kitchen."

Lieutenant Valcour wondered at this. The sound of one shot might well have been heard down in the kitchen: the shot which had killed Endicott and which had been fired from the balcony. The sound would surely have travelled clearly in the still night air and to the kitchen from outside. And yet he believed Nurse Vickers implicitly in her statement that she had heard no shot. There was no earthly reason why she should lie about it. The fact convinced him that whoever had fired had held the pistol inside of the window. He glanced at the sash and realized that the opening afforded plenty of room for a hand holding a gun to reach through.

"No," he said, "I suppose you couldn't have heard anything at all. Maybe Roberts can help me. She was in the room, wasn't she, when you came back?"

"Oh, yes, Lieutenant, and terribly excited about the shooting. She seemed so upset, in fact, that if there hadn't been so many much more important things for Dr. Worth to attend to, I'd have asked him to give her something to quiet her."

"One can hardly blame Roberts," Lieutenant Valcour said. "The fusillade must have been quite a shock, you know. And then everyone's nerves are on edge to-night anyway. In just what

fashion was she upset, Miss Vickers? From your professional experience, I mean, you probably could diagnose her actions. Was
it fright—nervous shock?"

"Oh, fright, of course, Lieutenant. I've seen lots of nervous
and hysterical people during my work but never one as badly off
as she was. I'm not exaggerating one bit when I say that she was
gripped with an hysterical sort of terror."

"Really. As bad as that?"

"Why, I was almost afraid even to let her stay in the room
with the patient. The poor creature actually seemed to blame
Mrs. Endicott in some fashion for what had happened. Just
imagine this, Lieutenant: when I came in she was literally leaning over the bed and shaking her fist at Mrs. Endicott."

"You are quite certain of this, Miss Vickers?"

"I saw it with my own eyes, Lieutenant."

"And was Roberts saying anything?"

"Just the jumble that people go in for when they're hysterical."

"You couldn't catch anything connected?"

"I didn't try, Lieutenant. I had to get her away from the bed
and calm her down."

"You were able to?"

"I was. She calmed down quite suddenly and became perfectly normal again. I persuaded her to run downstairs and make
herself a good bracing cup of tea."

"Possibly carrying the pistol with her," Lieutenant Valcour
thought bitterly, "to hide it in some place where it might never
be found."

"Did she come back into the room afterward?" he said.

"Well, not really, Lieutenant. I know how particular you police officers are about the littlest details. She just stopped at the

door to tell me she was feeling all right again. She said she was going upstairs to her room to take a little rest."

"And you're quite sure, Miss Vickers, that you can't recall any of the words that Roberts was saying when you found her leaning over the bed?"

"I would if I could, Lieutenant. It was just a jumble. Ice—something about 'ice and human hearts.' Then she switched to 'searing flames' and I don't know what all else."

"Would it bother you very much to go up to her room and see whether she's in condition to come down here for a few minutes?"

"Why, not at all. I'd be glad to."

"Thank you, Miss Vickers. You've helped me tremendously. Oh, there's just one thing, Miss Vickers."

Miss Vickers paused at the doorway.

"Yes, Lieutenant?"

"When you came back upstairs from the kitchen, did you notice anything about the atmosphere of Mrs. Endicott's room?"

"Why—I don't know—you mean a sense of tension or something?"

"No, I don't. I mean was it as warm as when you left it, or cooler, or what?"

"Yes, I do, too—it was cooler—*much.* Because I remember after I quieted Roberts I went over to one of the radiators to see if the heat was still turned on. I thought Roberts must have turned it off, although I couldn't for the life of me see why. But the radiator was quite hot, so I realized it must have been just the change from the kitchen. It's a hot kitchen."

"That is probably just what it was. Would you send Roberts to me now, please?"

"I will, Lieutenant."

"Thank you."

Miss Vickers went out and closed the door.

Lieutenant Valcour then did a rather horrible thing. He went over to the bed and pulled down enough of the sheet so that Endicott's face was exposed.

And then he sat down and waited for Roberts.

# CHAPTER XX
## 3:24 *a. m.*—On Private Heights

"You wanted to see me, Lieutenant?"

She *had* been under a strain, and a rather terrible one. There wasn't any doubt about that. It was emotion, after all, that brought age, not years, thought Lieutenant Valcour as he glanced at the dark rings so clearly visible beneath her tragic eyes.

Roberts hadn't looked toward the bed—yet—but then he hadn't really expected that she would. Perhaps she wouldn't look for some time, but eventually she would lose some portion of that really splendid self-control that she was exerting and then, instead of the expanse of white sheet she had been expecting, there would be Endicott's face. . . .

"I wonder if you could tell me, Miss Roberts, the number of shots that were fired during the shooting."

"I'm sure I couldn't."

She was pointedly on guard, her eyes held at a level that included his cravat but went no higher.

"The question isn't as silly a one as it seems," Lieutenant Valcour said. "I don't suggest for a minute that you counted the

shots as they were being fired, actually, but it's quite within possibility that your subconscious mind really did that very thing,
and that on consciously thinking about it the number might
come to you. It's something along the principle of visualizing
sound."

"I'm sorry. I'm sure that no amount of thinking about it
would clear the rather terrible confusion of that moment."

"Won't you sit down?"

"I prefer to stand, thank you."

"Just as you wish. You were with Mrs. Endicott, weren't you,
when it happened?"

"Yes."

Lieutenant Valcour admired the accomplished ease with
which the word had so unhesitatingly been brought out; but
then most women, in his estimation, were natural-born liars.
The art formed for him one of their greatest charms.

"You were sitting down beside the bed?" he went on.

"Yes. Reading."

Splendid—splendid—she was a Bernhardt—a Duse.

"And Miss Vickers?"

"She was down in the kitchen making some coffee."

"Did the shooting upset you, Miss Roberts?"

"I'm naturally nervous. The sound of firing has always disturbed me terribly." Then she flung at him abruptly, "My brother
was killed in the war."

Lieutenant Valcour both looked and felt genuinely consoling.
He also felt a selfish measure of irritation. The statement was
such a perfect period mark. When a young woman, no matter how great a criminal, potentially, announces flatly that her
brother has been killed during the war, one can't ride over the
fact roughshod.

"Was there anyone whom you loved killed in the war, Lieutenant?"

She was determined to hammer at the point, it seemed. He wished that she would stop.

"There wasn't, Miss Roberts."

"Then you don't know much about soldiers.'"

"No, not much, really."

"I don't mean soldiers—or the war itself, either. It's a state of being—a sort of lucid abnormality. It's hard to tell you just what I do mean. But it's the thing," she ended fiercely, "that made me understand Mr. Endicott. He never quite recovered, you see, from being a soldier."

"And perhaps it also made you understand why Mrs. Endicott misunderstood him?"

Things were going better now; the channel was broadening into useful seas.

"Of course it was," Roberts said. "She, too, lost no one in the war."

The fog rolled in again.

"I'm afraid I'm not following you very clearly."

"It's quite useless, Lieutenant—simply that in Mr. Endicott I kept seeing my brother. I suffered for him to the extent I would have suffered for my brother had my brother been in similar circumstances."

"Suffered?"

"Yes, suffered. From her damned superiority."

"You think that Mrs. Endicott overdid the mental?"

He noted that Roberts was slowly losing control. There was a blazing quality of anger creeping into her eyes.

"Lieutenant, she regarded that man as her tame tiger. You realize how strong he must have been physically."

"Very strong."

"It used to please her to control him—you know the way it's commonly expressed—with a 'word.'"

"I shouldn't exactly say that she had succeeded."

"The other women?"

"Yes."

"She didn't care about that. If anything, it satisfied her sense of power. She looked on them as a pack of shoddy substitutes that he could fool with, kick around, and treat terribly, if he liked. But she still remained the original—the unapproachable—the happy possessor of a tame tiger. He was always *hers*, you see, no matter what it was he had done. She's had him crying."

"That's a little hard to believe."

"It's the truth. He took her in his hands one night and twisted her—just like that! She didn't say a thing to him. For a month afterward he went around the house like a whipped cat. Then she said something kind to him, and he cried. I wish she was in hell."

"Perhaps she is, Miss Roberts—just that."

"She won't stay in it long. Her kind doesn't."

Lieutenant Valcour held his eyes thoughtfully directed toward the bed.

"Tell me, Miss Roberts, do you think that Mr. Endicott is happier dead? Let me put it in this fashion: if Mr. Endicott had really been your brother, would you rather have seen him dead than living in the emotional hell you picture Mr. Endicott as having lived in?"

His gaze retained its determined fixity.

"No," she said. "There is always a way out." It was irresistible.

She found herself having to look, too. Against every advice of instinct her eyes were drawn toward the bed in company with Lieutenant Valcour's . . . peace—there *was* peace—greater than she had ever seen when he had been living—peace to a tired heart—a plain, normal, happy human heart that had been broken on the wheel of too much complexity. . . . "Oh, I'm lying, Lieutenant! I would—I would—a million times rather."

He worked very fast now, having captured the mood. "Were you thinking of all that when you stood outside on the balcony and watched him through the window?"

Her eyes clung immovably to the cold closed lids, the mouth, carved in gentle shadows; her very being seemed withdrawn on private heights. "I wasn't on the balcony."

"And I'd like to know what you did with the gun."

. . . Perhaps he was laughing at it all now, if people laugh in heaven. He and her brother. They would have met and be laughing at it all together. But they wouldn't be laughing at her. . . . "There wasn't any need to use the gun, Lieutenant."

"Then what did you do with it?"

"Put it back in the bottom of my trunk." . . . He'd know, now, the exact reason why she had done the things that she had done. People know everything in heaven—sort of an enveloping awareness—like lightning darting brilliantly to immediate comprehension at its target—target—gun?—*gun*. Her face was bleak ivory. "What did you say, Lieutenant?"

"I had just asked you, Miss Roberts, what you did with the gun, and you told me that you put it back again in the bottom of your trunk."

Her eyes, as she looked at him, were strangely devoid of fear.

"Then if I told you that, you'll find it there."

"It wasn't the wisest place to put it, Miss Roberts."

"It doesn't matter much."

"You mean you don't care?"

"Not just that. I'm speaking about the gun. I never fired it."

"Then why did you hide it?"

"Because it's illegal to have a gun."

"Then why did you have one, Miss Roberts?"

"It's one my brother gave me over twelve years ago. I've always kept it with me."

"What calibre is it?"

"A Colt .38."

The bullet in Lieutenant Valcour's pocket had been fired from a Colt .38.

"And to-night you were going to use it to save Mr. Endicott by shooting him."

"No, Lieutenant. I was going to use it to shoot Mrs. Endicott if she attempted to get near him again."

"Again?"

"Why, yes, Lieutenant. She went out of the room last night right after he had knocked and said good-bye."

"Out into the hallway?"

"Yes."

"When did she come back?"

"She didn't come back."

"Then when was the next time you saw her?"

"When you rang for me—after you had found Mr. Endicott in the cupboard."

"And you think it was Mrs. Endicott who put him there." Lieutenant Valcour thought for a moment of the broken finger nail of Mrs. Endicott's otherwise immaculate hand. "But why, Miss Roberts, should she kill her—tiger?"

"Perhaps Mr. Hollander could tell you that better than I."

"And why did you get a gun to prevent Mrs. Endicott from going again to her husband, when you knew she was under the influence of a narcotic, that she was unconscious, and couldn't possibly move?"

"Because, Lieutenant, she never drank the narcotic."

# CHAPTER XXI
## 3:51 *a. m.*—A Woman's Slipper

LIEUTENANT VALCOUR felt a distinct shock, and his eyes became predatorily alert. If this astonishing thing was true and Mrs. Endicott had not taken the narcotic prepared for her by Dr. Worth, then the bypaths one might dart along were numerous and alarming indeed.

"How do you know, Miss Roberts?" he said.

"Because when the nurse went downstairs to make that coffee I went over to the bed. I wanted to take a close look at Mrs. Endicott. Have you ever felt that desire to look closely at something that you hate very much? It's the curiosity of hate, I suppose. I put my hand on the spread, at the edge, so that I could lean down. The spread was damp; something had been poured on it. There wasn't anything that could have been poured on it except the narcotic. She'd recovered consciousness, you see, when the nurse and Dr. Worth brought her in from here and put her to bed."

"But wouldn't he or the nurse have seen her pour it out?"

"None of us saw it, Lieutenant, because she said, just after the doctor had handed her the glass, 'There's blood on that dresser.'

We all looked at the dresser, of course. Naturally there wasn't any blood on it. The doctor thought she was delirious. She was just finishing drinking when we turned around."

"Didn't you accuse her—when you felt the damp spot on the spread?"

"What was the use? She never would have admitted it. I believe," Roberts said fiercely, "that I could have stuck pins in her and that she'd have endured the pain rather than admit it. And suddenly I began to feel afraid—not so much of her, as of what she might do to Mr. Endicott. She was playing a trick and I didn't know just what the purpose of it was. I ran upstairs and got my gun, then came right back."

"She was still in bed?"

"Yes. But the shooting was over, and the room was cold. The room was cold"—Roberts's voice was very intense as she drove her points home—"and her skin was cold, and her breathing was heavy from recent exertion. I think I was going to kill her. I *would* have killed her if the nurse hadn't come in just then."

"Why didn't you tell someone of this at once, Miss Roberts?"

"Would you have? Would anyone have?"

"I don't quite understand."

"There had just been that shooting—and I had a gun. I wanted to get rid of it. By the time I had got rid of it, it was too late. I couldn't say anything then without practically accusing myself of a murder I didn't commit."

"You'll stay here in the house, Miss Roberts?"

"Naturally, since I'm to be accused of having killed Mr. Endicott."

"Not as yet, Miss Roberts."

"It won't bother me." She added bitterly, as she started for the door, "You'll find me a tractable prisoner."

"One minute please, Miss Roberts. How long were you gone from Mrs. Endicott's room when you went upstairs to get the gun?"

"Just long enough to run up and back again. I have no idea, really."

"Where is your room?"

"On the upper floor—the room to the left of the corridor in the front of the house."

"And whereabouts did you keep the gun?"

"In my trunk—where it is now."

"Was the trunk locked?"

"Yes. I keep it locked."

"And the keys for it?"

"In a purse. The purse was in a dresser drawer."

"Then that gives us a pretty good idea of the length of time you must have been gone, doesn't it?"

"I suppose it does. Three or four minutes, probably."

"Nearer, I imagine, to five or six. But we don't require the actual number of minutes. The point we need is, rather, a comparison of two different operations within the same time limit. While you were going through the various movements you have described, would Mrs. Endicott have had the time to get out of bed, supply herself with a revolver, open a window, and, from the balcony, shoot Mr. Endicott, return to her room, and be in bed again by the time you came down? I think so, don't you?"

"There would have been plenty of time for that."

"You've been with Mrs. Endicott for quite a while. Have you ever noticed whether or not she owns a pistol?"

"I don't think I have. No, I'm sure I've never seen one. That doesn't prove anything, though. There are any number of private places where she may have kept it. It is also possible"—Roberts seemed desperately earnest in her effort to strengthen each link in her accusation, for she was accusing rather than simply offering a theory—"that someone may recently have given her a revolver, isn't it?"

"Everything is possible."

"Mr. Hollander, for example?"

"A very good example."

He said nothing further, and after a while the stillness became almost physically oppressive. Roberts was finished with emotions. "Is that all?" she said, and her voice was colourless.

"I believe so, Miss Roberts—except that I wish you would tell me why, in view of your recent insinuations concerning Mrs. Endicott and Hollander, you ever suggested him as the proper friend to stay with her husband to-night. It's a little inconsistent, don't you think?"

"Very."

"Then why did you do it?"

"I have nothing further to say."

Lieutenant Valcour went abruptly to the door and opened it. Cassidy and Hansen were standing near by in the corridor.

"Hansen," he said, "go with Miss Roberts up to her room. There is a gun in her trunk. She will give it to you. Keep it for me."

"Yes, sir."

Roberts went outside.

"Am I to consider myself under arrest, Lieutenant?"

"No, Miss Roberts. But, as I have explained, you are not to leave the house. Cassidy, come inside here with me."

Cassidy came in and closed the door. He watched Lieutenant Valcour draw the sheet up again over Endicott's face.

"What's Dr. Worth doing, Cassidy?"

"He has gone back to bed, sir. Shall I go get him?" Cassidy cast one suspicious look toward the bed.

"No, let him sleep. There's nothing just this instant. I'll want to see him in about a quarter of an hour, though."

Lieutenant Valcour went into the bathroom, opened the window, and went outside onto the balcony. The gray before dawning was in the sky, and a rare clearness was vibrant in the fresh, sweet air.

The outline of the garden down below was quite distinct. There were other gardens belonging to the adjacent houses, too, and to the houses backing them from the rear. It was a street of gardens which bloomed, Lieutenant Valcour reflected, for the express benefit of caretakers in summer, while their owners spent the season at fashionable resorts either in the mountains or on the shore.

Lieutenant Valcour went and carefully examined with his flashlight the window to Endicott's room that had been raised from the bottom when the shot was fired. He played the light upon the surface of its glass. It was quite clean. There was no trace of any pressing of noses or of foreheads against its polished surface. Nor, on the stone sill, were there any telltale threads of silk, or any of the various clues that would serve to indicate a woman's presence.

He stared speculatively for a minute at the windows of the room above, where the curiously vindictive Mrs. Siddons was now presumably resting, or else indulging in her blank-eyed game of mental maledictions. No, he couldn't really visualize her as descending to the balcony by a rope or any other kind of ladder. A hundred years ago, perhaps, she might have gone so far as to shape a replica of Mr. Endicott in wax and then, with appropriate incantations, proceed to stick pins in such portions of it as would cabalistically do the most good. But there was no such simple expedient left her in our modern skeptic age. It would be necessary, of course, to interview her further concerning those vague, bitter hints she had thrown out about outrageous actions on the part of Endicott toward the maids.

Even the city could not kill the fair fresh breezes of dawn. He stared at the dimming stars and wondered whether Roberts's extraordinary statement was a lie. For after all it hinged upon nothing more significant than a damp spot at the edge of a spread, and Roberts could easily have spilled something there herself to offer as corroborative evidence to her tale. Was she, he wondered, quite so smart? And from all that he had been able to judge of her, he rather thought that she was.

He would have to consult with Dr. Worth, of course, before doing anything drastic. And the doctor would probably raise a holler, especially since he had just gone to bed and would have to be yanked summarily out of it again. Well, bed-yankings were to be expected in the lives of doctors and of the police; they were expected to be perpetually on tap, like heat or water.

He made his way slowly toward the windows of Mrs. Endicott's room, carefully inspecting the balcony and sills with his flashlight as he went along. There were no smudges, no threads, no clues until he reached the last window in the row. And there, on the balcony floor just below its sash, something blazed in the circle of his torch a bright jade green.

It was a woman's slipper.

# CHAPTER XXII
## 4:14 *a. m.*—Tap—Tap—Tap

Lieutenant Valcour picked the slipper up and sighed. It was a distressingly leading and decisive clue, but it did not lead in a direction he cared to follow, nor did it decide things as he thought they ought to be decided.

On the surface of it, the case seemed blatantly plain: Hollander had come to the house at seven to save Mrs. Endicott from committing murder or suicide and had shocked Endicott almost to death—and just a short while ago Mrs. Endicott had shot her husband to prevent him from making a statement that would convict Hollander.

Rubbish!

Lieutenant Valcour flatly refused to believe it. And yet one had to believe that Hollander had certainly intended to stab Endicott with that knife; the point was irrefutable. Furthermore, Hollander's motives remained clear enough and beautifully simple: he wanted to protect Mrs. Endicott.

But what about her motives?

And Roberts's?

And as a kernel to the whole perplexing enigma, what had

been the object of the search through Endicott's pockets and among the papers in the left-hand upper drawer of his desk?

There was nothing to be gained, however, by standing outside on the balcony and admiring the flushing sky and breathing in with the manner of a connoisseur the morning air. Lieutenant Valcour returned, via the bathroom window, to Endicott's room.

"The night's almost over, Lieutenant," said Cassidy by way of greeting.

"Almost over, Cassidy."

"And it's been a hell of a night, too, if you don't mind my saying it."

"I don't mind your saying it."

"Especially for him."

Cassidy jerked a muscular thumb toward the bed.

"Least of all for him, Cassidy."

"He may be well out of it at that."

"He is. There's a lot of beautiful tripe written about how all people kill the things they love. Metaphysically, perhaps. But with a bullet, Cassidy? Not so."

"I don't get you, Lieutenant."

"That isn't strange, Cassidy. So far I don't even get myself."

Lieutenant Valcour went to the door and opened it. Hansen was standing outside, and in his hand was a gun wrapped in a clean handkerchief.

"Roberts's gun, Hansen?"

"Yes, Lieutenant. It was just where you said it would be, in the trunk. I wrapped it in a handkerchief to keep any prints you might want on it."

"That's right, Hansen. Go upstairs now and wake up Dr. Worth. Ask him if he will please come down here at once."

"Yes, Lieutenant." Hansen hesitated for a minute.

"Well, what is it, Hansen?"

"I understood you all right didn't I, sir," Hansen said uncomfortably, "when you told me that maid wasn't to be put under arrest?"

"Yes. I don't want to do anything about her as yet. Later on we may book her on a violation of the Sullivan Law and again we may not."

"Yes, sir."

Lieutenant Valcour took the gun and went back into the room with it, closing the door. He carefully unfolded enough of the handkerchief so that the barrel was exposed. He sniffed this and decided that the gun had neither been recently fired nor cleaned. There was just the definite odourlessness which one finds with guns that have not been used or taken care of for a very long time. So far, then, he was inclined to believe that Roberts's story was correct.

"Is that the rod that done the trick, Lieutenant?" said Cassidy, who had been keenly interested in the sniffings.

"No, it isn't, Cassidy. This gun hasn't been fired for years, maybe."

"Well, I wish it was. I'd like to get out of this joint."

"Still nervous, Cassidy?"

"No, I ain't nervous, Lieutenant. I'm just uncomfortable. It's like there was something in this case that hasn't broken yet. You know what I mean? Something we ain't so much as put a finger on."

Lieutenant Valcour knew very well just exactly what Cassidy meant. He, too, felt that same indefinable effect of impending "somethings" that were connected with obscure danger. It was an emotion, however, which required official scowlings. After all, psychic patrolmen were not considered as being to the best

interests of the force. One shouldn't be allowed, really, to graduate into psychic realms anywhere below the rank of lieutenant.

"Discounting your weekly adventures between paper covers,
this is your first real murder case, isn't it, Cassidy?"

"I thank God it is, sir."

"Well, you'll get used to them after a while. Before you're
called in on your fourth or fifth you'll be finished with having
presentiments."

"Will they be likely to be like this one, sir?"

"That will depend entirely, Cassidy, upon just how much
publicity this one is given in the papers, as well as on the supply
at hand of potential victims who have weak hearts. I dare say
the method will become fashionable for a while." There was a
peevish rap on the door. "Ah, come in, Doctor."

Dr. Worth was just as peevish as his knock. The camel's-hair
dressing gown in which he was still bundled hinted blurringly
at indignant muscles that quivered beneath its loose folds. His
hair was rumpled-looking and frowsy.

"Really, Lieutenant," he began, "this is getting to be beyond
a joke."

"I'm sorry, Doctor, but I had to discuss Mrs. Endicott's condition with you most seriously and at once."

Dr. Worth paled a little at this.

"Nothing's happened to her, too, has there?"

"No, Doctor, nothing has. And I don't think that just now I
could stand another murder. It's about her physical condition in
general. Is her heart all right?"

Dr. Worth's curiosity was beginning to get the upper hand
over his grouch.

"Perfectly sound. Why do you ask?"

"Because I want to try an experiment on her."

"You want to what, sir?" Dr. Worth almost shouted it. He was thoroughly awake now.

"Not so loud, please, Doctor. I want you to let me stay in the room alone with your patient. You can open the connecting bathroom door a little and watch me through its crack, but I want the nurse out of the way. And I don't want you to make any noise or comments while you're watching. I don't want Mrs. Endicott to know that you're there."

Dr. Worth looked at Lieutenant Valcour sharply. "This is nonsense. She couldn't possibly tell who was or who wasn't there. She's unconscious."

"Perhaps she isn't, Doctor. This is what her maid has just told me." Lieutenant Valcour offered Dr. Worth Roberts's astonishing theory concerning the poured-out narcotic, and Dr. Worth was quite properly astonished. "So you see it's a possibility, Doctor, and the fact of my finding that slipper outside of the window makes it practically a certainty."

"It's the most astounding thing I've ever heard of in my life. If you don't intend to shock her, Lieutenant, I'll agree to anything you say."

"I shan't do anything rough, Doctor, like discharging a gun off near her ear, or pinching her, or slapping her, or any of the tricks which are so popularly supposed to be kept up the sleeve of a policeman. You can stop me at any minute if you object to anything I may be doing."

"Have you planned just what you will do?"

"With a woman like Mrs. Endicott there wouldn't be any use in planning anything. All that I can do in advance is to create an atmosphere and then do whatever occurs to me as being best when the proper time comes. There won't be anything complicated about it."

"Just what sort of an atmosphere, Lieutenant?"

"Well, in the first place I'll call the nurse outside into the corridor and you can tell her not to go back in again until I say so. You might suggest to her that she go down to the kitchen and make some coffee—she seems a little dippy about coffee—or something. Then we'll leave Mrs. Endicott quite alone in her room for a minute or two. If she's really faking, she'll begin to worry about what is going on. Then the door will open again and, instead of the nurse, I'll come in. She'll be pretty certain to suspect that I've found the slipper, but will be all the more careful to keep up her pretence of being under the influence of the narcotic. If she gets away with that, you know, she can always claim that Roberts herself must have dropped the slipper onto the balcony as a plant. The main thing is that Mrs. Endicott won't know just what's up, and when a woman of her temperament can't figure a thing out mentally, it about drives her crazy."

"Then I suppose, Lieutenant, that when you get her into this receptive state you'll speak to her?"

Lieutenant Valcour laughed. "On the contrary, Doctor, I haven't the slightest intention of saying a single word. Shall we go now? After you've arranged things with Nurse Vickers you can come back in here again and start watching from the bathroom."

They went outside, and Lieutenant Valcour rapped softly on Mrs. Endicott's door. It opened a bit, and Nurse Vickers looked out. She saw Dr. Worth and came outside, shutting the door behind her.

"You wanted to see me, Doctor?"

"Yes, Miss Vickers. How is Mrs. Endicott?"

"Quite comfortable, Doctor. She's breathing as peacefully as a child."

"There haven't been any signs of restlessness?"

"Oh, no, Doctor. She hasn't budged since I've been watching her."

Dr. Worth mildly raised his eyebrows. "That in itself is rather curious," he said.

"Curious, Doctor?"

"Oh, nothing to be alarmed at, Miss Vickers. You look a little tired. Run downstairs and drink some coffee. The lieutenant, here, will stay with Mrs. Endicott, and you're not to go back into her room again until he says so."

"Help!" thought Lieutenant Valcour. As a detective Dr. Worth was a darned fine doctor. Miss Vickers, as he had expected, was instantly curious.

"Something more wrong, Doctor?"

"No Miss Vickers," Lieutenant Valcour said coldly. "Please do as the doctor instructed, and at once."

"Oh."

Nurse Vickers, feeling a little outraged, vanished toward the stairs.

"Shall I go and stand by the bathroom door now?" said Dr. Worth.

"If you wish. Don't make the slightest sound when you're opening it, and don't open it more than an inch at the most, please."

"I won't, Lieutenant."

Dr. Worth, feeling very much like one of those fabulous characters he had read about in Fenimore Cooper when a child, went back into Endicott's room.

Lieutenant Valcour waited another full minute before he opened the door and went inside. He did not look at Mrs. Endicott, but walked softly over to a chair, lifted it, and placed it close beside the bed. He drew the slipper from his pocket and sat down.

There was an utter and complete hush. For three minutes—he timed himself with his wrist watch—he sat motionless and stared at the closed lids of Mrs. Endicott's eyes.

Then he began to tap the slipper quite softly, but quite persistently and with a rhythmic regularity, upon an arm of the chair.

Tap—tap—tap—tap—tap——

Mrs. Endicott's face retained the smooth expressionlessness of slumber.

Tap—tap—tap——

Her breathing held the steady depths of sleep.

Tap—tap—tap—tap——

"If you do that much longer," she said quietly, "I shall go insane."

# CHAPTER XXIII
## 4:29 *a. m.*—A Turn of the Screw

"You NEEDN'T say anything you don't care to, Mrs. Endicott."

"I'm glad you didn't use the stereotyped formula, Lieutenant. It would have disappointed me if you had. Get me a cigarette, please; there are some over there on the dresser."

Lieutenant Valcour stood up. He got the cigarettes and lighted one for Mrs. Endicott and one for himself.

"You shouldn't have dropped your slipper outside of the window," he said.

"You shouldn't have found it."

Her eyes, now that they were opened, were admirably guarded, and her fingers, as they held the cigarette, showed no trace of nervousness.

"The slipper is of no great consequence, Mrs. Endicott. There are so many other things, too, you see."

"Sort of a wholesale strewing of clues? I never imagined you as bothering very much with clues. It's people you're more interested in: reading their minds."

Her eyes offered an almost impudent invitation that he read hers.

"Whom were you aiming at when you fired, Mrs. Endicott, at your husband or at Mr. Hollander?"

Mrs. Endicott blew smoke rings elaborately.

"At neither, Lieutenant. I didn't have a gun."

"Then it was just curiosity?"

"What was?"

"Your going out on the balcony."

"I didn't go out on the balcony. I've never been on it in my life."

"I am not stupid, Mrs. Endicott."

"Nor very credulous, either."

"No, nor credulous."

"That's the trouble with truth: it often sounds so silly."

"Surely you realize how things look against you, Mrs. Endicott."

"Black."

"The worst of all is your not having taken the narcotic, and then having pretended to be in a state of unconsciousness."

Her eyes became stupefyingly innocent. "Is it illegal to decide not to take medicine, Lieutenant?"

His respect for her as an adversary began to mount by leaps and bounds. "No, Mrs. Endicott. But in the present case it was purposefully deceptive."

"Why, I simply disliked hurting Dr. Worth's feelings; that was all."

Lieutenant Valcour pictured her maintaining that attitude—smartly dressed in becomingly plain black, very innocent, very beautiful-looking—before the twelve impressionable and normally dumb people one finds on juries. He was grudgingly afraid she could get away with it.

"And it isn't illegal, either," she went on, "to go to sleep, is it?"

Lieutenant Valcour decided that if anything was to be gained from the interview he would have to give a turn to the screw.

"No, Mrs. Endicott, sleeping isn't illegal. Even," he added negligently, "if your husband has just been killed, and your—well, whatever state of relationship exists between you and Mr. Hollander—your friend, let us say, is wounded to the point of death."

The cigarette dropped from her fingers to the floor. Lieutenant Valcour crushed it with the sole of his shoe.

"I don't believe you."

Her voice had the same pallid qualities as her skin.

"You must have seen for yourself, Mrs. Endicott, that he was pretty badly hurt when he slipped to the floor. There was blood enough smeared around, goodness knows."

"You're trying to trap me."

"Just stating facts, Mrs. Endicott. Of course you may have left the instant after you fired and so not have seen Mr. Hollander shot down by the police."

"You are being vulgarly brutal."

"You were certainly in a frantic enough hurry to have dropped your slipper and not to have bothered to pick it up. Did you throw the gun into the garden, Mrs. Endicott? We're bound to find it, you know."

"Is Mr. Hollander still in the house?"

"No."

"Where have they taken him?"

"To the hospital."

"Please ring for my maid and leave the room. I must go to him immediately."

"I'm sorry."

"Will you please leave this room?"

"You don't seem to realize, Mrs. Endicott, that you are under arrest."

The thought stunned her. Her head fell back among the pillows as if it had been thrown there.

"But that's silly—silly, I tell you."

"You admitted yourself, Mrs. Endicott, that the truth is always silly."

"You are actually charging me with the murder of my husband?"

"'Arrest' was perhaps an injudicious word. I am holding you, Mrs. Endicott, as a material witness, for the present."

Mrs. Endicott had recovered somewhat from the shock.

"I shan't be bromidic, Lieutenant, and attempt either tears or bribery. I'm not stupid enough to think that either would affect you in the slightest from the performance of duty. But I should like to appeal to your reason."

"You will find me a sympathetic listener, Mrs. Endicott. My wretched conceit forces me to add that I shall also be an intelligent one."

"You see, I knew pretty well what was going on from hearing the nurse and Roberts talking about it. Lieutenant, just what do you want me to admit?"

"That you were on the balcony."

"But I wasn't."

"Then how did your slipper get there?"

"It fell from my foot."

Lieutenant Valcour stood up abruptly. "You will have to pardon me, Mrs. Endicott," he said, "while I search this room."

"You misunderstand me. I mean exactly what I say. I wasn't on the balcony, and the slipper did fall off my foot. If you must know it, I was straddling the window sill."

"What stopped you from going out, Mrs. Endicott?"

"The sound of the shooting. It unnerved me. I almost fell back into the room and closed the window. I knew that I had dropped a slipper outside, but the idea of doing anything further than hurrying back into bed terrified me."

Lieutenant Valcour examined the slipper he still held in his hand. "This is a slipper for the left foot," he said. "And in that case, when you were straddling the window it is the foot which must have been on the outside. Isn't that so?"

"That's rather elementary, isn't it?"

"Quite. But it serves to prove that at the moment when the shots were fired you could look along the balcony toward the windows of your husband's room. Did you?"

"I imagine so. I'm not quite certain, really. It was absolutely dark out there."

"On the contrary, there was a glow cast on the balcony from the farthest window, which was open a little, wasn't there?"

"Perhaps. Yes, I think there was."

"And did you see anybody standing at that window when the shots were fired?"

"You mean on the balcony?"

"Yes."

"No."

"That is all, Mrs. Endicott."

"You don't believe me."

"Frankly, I don't."

Mrs. Endicott's expression hardened perceptibly. Whether from bitterness or from some sudden private determination it was difficult to say.

"Does being detained as a material witness prohibit me from getting out of bed and dressing?" she said.

"Not at all. In fact, it is essential that you do so. You see, we detain our material witnesses in jail."

He heard again, as he had heard it earlier in the night, the muted echo of brass bells in her voice. "If you will leave me then, please?"

"Just as soon as I have searched the room."

"For what?"

"For a revolver, Mrs. Endicott."

Mrs. Endicott closed her eyes. She turned on her side and faced the wall. Lieutenant Valcour conducted his search with the thoroughness and speed born of experience. In the room, in the room's cupboard, in the various drawers, beneath the different pieces of furniture, there was no gun. He took a dressing gown and placed it on the bed.

"Put this on, please, Mrs. Endicott, I want to search the bed."

She did so, without either comment or objection. She went to the window and stared unseeingly at the breaking day.

Lieutenant Valcour removed the spread, and with a pencil roughly outlined the damp spot where the narcotic had been spilled. Then he folded the spread and tucked it under one arm. The rest of the bedclothes, the mattress, the pillows, concealed no gun. He walked to the door.

"I will send your maid to you, Mrs. Endicott, if you wish."

She continued to stare through the window and to present her back to him. She said nothing. He tried to catch the suggestion in her pose. It wasn't a gesture of petty rudeness or angry spite; nor was it by any means suggestive of despair or fear. He went outside and closed the door.

And as he crossed the corridor to Endicott's room it occurred to him with shocking clearness that, in spite of the idea's seeming absurdity, her pose had suggested a very definite mood of positive exaltation.

# CHAPTER XXIV

## 4:41 *a. m.*—As the Colours of Dawn

"Well," Lieutenant Valcour said, as he joined Dr. Worth in Endicott's room, "what do you think now?"

Dr. Worth was finished with bewilderments. In spite of the camel's-hair robe swathing him, he had recaptured to an impressive extent his air of dignity.

"Lieutenant," he said, "I think that my services are no longer required in this house. With your permission, I shall dismiss the two nurses and go home."

"Why, certainly, Doctor, if you wish. The prosecuting attorney will probably require your testimony to secure an indictment and will want you later on at the trial, but I'm sure he will bother you just as little as possible. We realize how annoying any court work is to a doctor."

"I shall be glad to testify whenever required."

"Will you also let me know where to keep in touch with the two nurses? Their testimony will be needed, too."

Dr. Worth stated the name and address of the Nurses' Home at which Miss Vickers and Miss Murrow could always be reached, and Lieutenant Valcour wrote them down in his note-book.

"Would it bother you very much, Lieutenant, to let Mrs. Endicott know that I have gone, when you see her?"

"Not at all, Doctor."

"I doubt whether she will require my services again." He paused for a moment at the doorway. "That woman, sir, is of iron."

"I shouldn't wonder, Doctor. At any rate, she is pretty thoroughly encased in metal. I'll send Cassidy along with you to pass you and the nurses by O'Brian down at the door. No one can leave the house, you see, without permission."

"Thank you, Lieutenant. Good-bye."

"Good-bye, Doctor, and thanks for all your assistance. Cassidy, come back after you've seen the doctor out, and stay in the corridor. I'll call when I need you."

"Yes, sir."

The door closed, and Lieutenant Valcour was alone. With a persistence that was becoming annoying, the same curious feeling of lurking danger crept out at him from the room's stillnesses. His nerves were usually as steady as the quality reputed to be enjoyed by a rock, and the strange little jumpings they were going in for were getting that fabulous animal known as his goat.

He went over to the chair before the flat-topped desk and sat down. There was that drawer filled with disordered papers to be gone through. He removed the drawer and emptied it of its contents by the simple expedient of turning it upside down onto the top of the desk.

There were, mixed up among bills and receipts, a surprising number of letters from women. He read each one of them carefully and felt a little sorrier, at the conclusion of each, for the future of the race—not so much because of any danger to its morals as to its mentality.

He made a little group of each batch of notes from the same woman. One pile topped the list with the number of ten. These were signed "Bebe" and were addressed with deplorable monotony to "My cave man." Endicott must have been rather an ass, he decided, as well as a pretty low sort of an animal. It was all very well for Roberts to rave on about soldiers, and simple hearts, and war, and things. That's just what it amounted to: raving. What if Endicott and, presumably, her brother had had simple hearts. So had guinea pigs.

Lieutenant Valcour wondered whether everyone else connected with the case was quite sane and he just a little mad. Roberts—Mrs. Endicott—the housekeeper—Hollander—Madame Velasquez. They all seemed a little touched, and that was a sign of madness when one considered everyone else but one's self insane. But no one was ever truly normal under disagreeable and terrifying circumstances; at least, he had never found anyone who was so.

The letters were meaningless as possible clues to a motive; just a sticky conglomeration of lust, greed, dullness, and execrable taste. He shoved them aside.

He watched the strengthening light of day as it came through the window across the desk before him. Such sky as he saw was of rubbed emerald, and the backs of the houses across the intervening gardens were mauve and dark gray, with lines of lemon yellow running thinly along their roofs.

He thought of *Bohême*—dawn always made him think of *Bohême*—and hummed a bar or two of it softly. Then he thought of Mrs. Endicott, and his thoughts were pastelled in the colours of the dawn: a woman of half-tones and overlapping lacquer shades.

It became quite clear in his mind that she never would have killed her husband. Or Hollander. That, in fact, she never would have killed anybody at all. The belief became fixed, even in face of the sizeable amount of evidence against her.

He reviewed her case, in digest, as the prosecuting attorney might present it to a jury: from the very start there was that contrary fact of her having telephoned for the police. Why? On the slender ground of a pencilled note that might or might not have been a threat, and an instinctive premonition that her husband was in danger. The prosecution would thereupon interpolate a smart crack or two on the general subject of premonitions, fortune tellings, and the Ace of Spades. They would point out that people who committed crimes which were bound to be shortly discovered occasionallly got in touch with the police in order to use the gesture as a premise of their innocence.

There were her definite admissions of intent to kill her husband—her having left her bedroom immediately upon his having knocked and said good-bye—and her recent most damaging actions in regard to the narcotic and having been on the balcony.

Motive?

The prosecuting attorney could offer a thousand. The most prominent ones would include a jealous rage at her husband's easily proved peccadillos with other women and her own rather significant attitude toward Hollander. Yes, it would be only too possible for the prosecuting attorney to get a conviction against Mrs. Endicott, and to rope Hollander in as an accomplice. He'd want the weapon, though, to make the case complete. Lieutenant Valcour had forgotten about the weapon. He stood up, went to the door, and opened it. Hansen was standing outside, having taken his post there until Cassidy should come back from letting out Dr. Worth and the nurses.

"Hansen," Lieutenant Valcour said, "I want you to search the backyard for a revolver that may have been thrown there from the balcony. If you can't find it, search the two adjoining backyards, and the three in the rear as well. Don't wake up the people in the other houses, just get a stepladder and cross the party walls."

"Yes, sir."

"Report to me as soon as you've finished, or find anything."

"Yes, sir."

Lieutenant Valcour closed the door again. The revolver would clinch the case: Mrs. Endicott the principal, and Hollander the accomplice. What a sweet bunch of muck it would be, too. There were all sorts of sob angles: Hollander and Endicott as Damon and Pythias, brothers in arms during the war who were transformed through the vicious caprice of a siren into Cain and Abel. Or would Mrs. Endicott spatter the tabloids as a woman wronged who had by a reversal of the usual position of the sexes taken her just revenge beneath the legendary cloak of the unwritten law? If her lawyers were smart, she would. And they would be smart, too. She'd probably have the most impressive battery of legal guns that were procurable in the state lined up on her side.

It wasn't the gun only that Lieutenant Valcour wanted. There was something else. Endicott's hat: that was it. How did the person who had been caught in the cupboard fit in with Endicott's hat? The answer came to him with the sudden clearness that will enlighten a problem that the subconscious mind has been working on for some time. The hat was the final touch to the person's disguise. And the fact would pre-suppose a woman.

A man's hat would add immeasurably to any disguise adopted by a woman.

But which woman?

And why had his hat been in the cupboard?

And still there was no answer to the baffling question as to what had been the object of the search through Endicott's pockets and his papers. There was, of course, a perfectly plain and logically possible solution: the object or paper, whatever it was, had been found and had been carried off by the thief along with Endicott's hat and the top button from his overcoat. And if such were the case, just what that object or paper was might never be known.

For the fourth time since he had been sitting at the desk Lieutenant Valcour sniffed the air. There was a faint trace of scent—a curiously reminiscent odour—all but intangible, but which he was quite certain he had encountered in some different locality at some time during the night. It was only apparent when he sat at the desk, and the deduction was reached without too much mental labour that it must, hence, emanate from something connected with the desk. Perhaps that aperture from which he had pulled the drawer——

The telephone rang sharply. He drew the instrument to him across the top of the desk, and took the receiver from the hook.

The call came, he was informed, from Central Office.

# CHAPTER XXV
## 5:01 *a. m.*—Lunatic Vistas

THE REPORT from Central Office which Lieutenant Valcour received over the telephone contained one definitely useful piece of information: the person who had used the comb and brushes belonging to Endicott had been a blonde and was either a man or a woman with bobbed hair.

And Mrs. Endicott, Lieutenant Valcour reflected as he hung up the receiver, had blonde shingled hair.

And so, except for the shingling, did Hollander.

Roberts, on the other hand, had not.

And where, he wanted to know, was his inspiring confidence in the innocence of Mrs. Endicott now? Precisely where it had been before. His mind began to gibber. What *was* that curious scent, that trace of an aroma? What about Hollander's roommate: the young Southerner who preyed upon wealthy women in night clubs? Had Endicott evidence that Hollander was mixed up in similar jobs, and had Hollander come to steal it, or silence Endicott? Rats! And what were Marge Myles's address and telephone number doing in Mrs. Endicott's personal directory? And why had Mrs. Endicott been such a stupid liar as to say she had seen no one on the balcony at the time when the shots were fired, when the only apparent place from which the shot that had killed Endicott could have been fired was the balcony? . . . A knock-knock.

"Come in," he said.

Cassidy opened the door.

"There's an old dame downstairs, Lieutenant, who insisted on coming in. She wants to see you."

"Did she say who she was, Cassidy?"

"She did. And you can believe it or not, sir, but her name is Molasses."

Lieutenant Valcour made a desperate clutch at his scattering reason.

"By all means, Cassidy," he said, "show Mrs. Molasses right up."

Madame Velasquez, in the penetrating light of early morning, was beyond words. The intervening hours since Lieutenant Valcour had left her, wigless and talking to herself in her step-daughter's apartment, had unquestionably been ones of worry. As she came into the room Lieutenant Valcour motioned to Cassidy to wait outside and close the corridor door.

Over her black sequinned dress she had thrown an evening cape of blue satin edged with marabou, and on her wig rested a picture hat trimmed with plumes. Her eyes ignored the details of Endicott's room, of Endicott's body stretched beneath the sheet; ignored everything but Lieutenant Valcour, the man whom she had come to see.

"Marge is dead," she said.

Her voice still retained the curious qualities that made it suggest a scream.

Lieutenant Valcour wearily closed his eyes. One other murder would truly prove to be the straw with himself in the rôle of the already overladen camel.

"Sit down, Madame Velasquez," he said, "and tell me how it happened."

Madame Velasquez spread billows of blue satin and marabou into an armchair.

"I don't know how it happened," she said.

"Did you find her body in the apartment?"

"There ain't no body." Madame Velasquez then added, as her brittle little eyes glittered with a strange sort of conviction, "He made away with it."

"Who did, Madame Velasquez?"

"Herbert Endicott," she said.

For a startled moment Lieutenant Valcour stared sharply down curious vistas: *had* Endicott killed Marge Myles, perhaps having called for her just after she had written that note to her mother? He brought himself up shortly. Utter nonsense! Endicott was in this very room at the time when Marge Myles must have been writing that note and was himself in the process of being killed.

"That isn't possible, Madame Velasquez," he said quietly. "Endicott was himself attacked right here at about the time your stepdaughter must have been writing that note to you. That was at seven last evening—at the very moment he was to call for her at her apartment—and it must have been a little after seven when she wrote, as she states in the note that he hadn't come."

"No matter"—her beringed fingers fluttered extravagantly—"I feel certain he did it, and I want him punished and caught."

"But Mr. Endicott is dead, Madame Velasquez."

"That's what *you* say," she said.

Was he really, Lieutenant Valcour wondered, going mad? There seemed such terribly disturbing possibilities of fact in every absurd aspect on the case the woman facing him opened up. Who, after all, *had* identified Endicott? His wife, and that only by implication; his friend Hollander, again by implication; Roberts had seen the dead man's face, but she, in common with all the world, was mad; Dr. Worth—what proof was there that Dr. Worth *was* Dr. Worth, or that the telephone number given him by Mrs. Endicott had been Dr. Worth's? It could all have been arranged by some clever mob. . . .

"This is folly," he said abruptly, really more to convince himself than the nutlike face peering at him from the armchair. What he needed was sleep—just a couple of hours of good sleep. "Madame Velasquez, that body on the bed is Herbert Endicott. Now tell me as lucidly as you can, please, just why you say that Marge is dead."

Her little eyes began to glitter with rage. "I believe she has killed herself to spite me." The knotted paste jewels on her thin fingers quivered indignantly. "She did it to make me suffer," she added, "to *stint* me."

"Just so she wouldn't have to give you any more money," he suggested.

Madame Velasquez began to weep noisily. "What'll I do, Lieutenant—oh, what *will* I do?"

He continued to regard her through lazy eyes.

"Can't you find somebody else to take her place?" he said. "Somebody else to blackmail?"

"I ain't young. It's too *late*."

"Tut, tut, Madame Velasquez."

"No, I ain't. And unless it's a case like Marge's was, such rackets take looks."

"But surely such an intelligent and charming woman as you, Madame Velasquez"—he unearthed a trowel and laid it on pretty thick—"a woman of the world, surely you can think up other cases where the evidence or proof can be faked. You know very well that you never had any real or visible proof that Marge killed her husband in that canoe disaster, now, don't you?"

"I did, too, Lieutenant."

"Nonsense. If you really did, you'd have it with you and would show it to me."

She nibbled the bait slyly and refused it.

"I wouldn't, and I haven't. And," she said, "I want proof of that trollop's death. I'll get it if I have to drag the river myself."

Madame Velasquez jumped up and ran nervously to the door.

"Then you saw her drown herself, Madame Velasquez?"

"I saw nothing, but I know—I know—what must have been . . ."

She was out in the corridor and running for the stairs—a velvet virago in blue. Lieutenant Valcour ran out after her, and saw that Cassidy was blocking her way.

"Ring up the wagon, Cassidy, and have her booked as a material witness."

Madame Velasquez began to screech. "Don't touch me. Keep your dirty hands off me."

"Take her downstairs, Cassidy, After you've arranged for the wagon leave her with O'Brian. Then go up to the housekeeper's room and ask Mrs. Siddons if she'll come down. I'll see her in Endicott's room."

"Yes, sir."

Lieutenant Valcour slowly retraced his steps When he was again in Endicott's room and the door shut, he felt a strong recurrence of that annoying sense of some hovering danger. He even shivered a little as if at some draught of cold air and glanced hastily at the windows.

But both were closed.

# CHAPTER XXVI
## 5:25 *a. m.*—There Was a Sailor

Mrs. Siddons had not gone to bed at all. She remained the same amazing pencil done in flat planes of black that had left him standing with his ear pressed against the panels of her bedroom door.

Lieutenant Valcour was acutely interested in her attitude toward Endicott's body. Her glance, the instant she entered the room, had flown to it surely and accurately. There was no sorrow, no horror or fear of the dead in that glance. It was wholly one of triumph, the satisfied gazing of some revenge that was removed from petty commonplaces. Mirrored in its satisfaction were avenging hell fires, tormenting presumably the black and wicked soul of what had been a very black and wicked Endicott. After that single initial glance she did not look toward the bed again, but came over and sat with extraordinary rigidity on the edge of a chair from where she could stare out of the window at the clear morning light of the winter's day.

"Several hours ago, Mrs. Siddons," Lieutenant Valcour said abruptly, "you spoke with considerable bitterness about Mr. Endicott's attitude toward the servants. I shan't embarrass you by asking for any information in detail. There are only one or two things that I want to know—— Are you listening to me, please?"

She dragged her eyes from the daylight, from the white misty air from which she had been gathering in her thoughts the happy flowers of a seed long bedded in hate.

"I am listening," she said.

"Then the first thing I want to know is this: was there any one particular instance in which Mr. Endicott's actions toward one of the servants were especially brutal or resented?"

The coals began to glow faintly beneath the ash that dusted her eyes.

"There was one very particular instance, Lieutenant."

"Recently, Mrs. Siddons?"

"It occurred about a year ago, almost to a day."

"Did Mr. Endicott attack her?"

"Yes."

"Here in the house?"

"No, Lieutenant. It happened on her afternoon and evening out. Mr. Endicoott's car was parked outside at the curb. He offered her a ride."

"Where is this girl now, Mrs. Siddons?"

"She was committed last year to an institution for the insane."

The ash was completely gone now, and her eyes blazed with avenging fires.

"But surely she brought charges, Mrs. Siddons?"

"She was insane when they found her, Lieutenant. She was trying to die by throwing herself in front of a motor in Central Park. She has never spoken lucidly since."

Lieutenant Valcour shrugged hopelessly. There it was again: that wretched wave of hearsay showing its baffling crest above the placid sea of established fact. Rumour had had it that Marge Myles had killed her husband; rumour now would have it about all sorts of terrible implications concerning Endicott, who was dead, and a girl who was confined in an insane asylum. And neither, obviously, could give direct testimony in accusation or defense.

"What was Mr. Endicott's story?" he said.

"That he had driven her to Macy's, where she wanted to buy something, and had left her there."

And why not? Undoubtedly Endicott had been the blackest sort of a sheep, but the case was valueless without a thousand illuminative lights, without a whole medical history of the girl's family, for example.

"Did you know this girl fairly well, Mrs. Siddons?"

"Yes. It is my habit to know all of the girls in my charge here very well. It is my duty, as I see it, to act not only as a house-keeper, but as their religious mentor and guide."

"Then in the case of this girl, had she ever previously shown any symptoms of being mentally unbalanced?"

"There were times when I thought so, yes. Her family, you see, was not free from the taint. Her grandmother, on her mother's side, had been insane. That is what made Mr. Endicott's actions so peculiarly detestable, sir. She might have continued to live a normal, useful, happy life had he not shocked her so fatally."

And on the other hand, Lieutenant Valcour decided, End-icott need not necessarily have done anything remotely of the sort. With such a direct strain of insanity inherent in her blood no outside agency whatever might have been needed to awak-en it into activity. And then, he reminded himself, the girl had been shopping. He often wondered why more women didn't go mad while shopping.

"Had Mr. Endicott any alibi for the period between the time he left her at Macy's and came home?"

"No, Lieutenant. He said he had driven out a ways on Long Island along the Motor Parkway and then had come back."

"So nothing was done about the matter officially?"

"There was nothing to do."

"Then the only substantiated fact in the story is that she was seen getting into Mr. Endicott's car in front of this house. I suppose someone did see her?"

"Yes."

"Who?"

"Mrs. Endicott saw her, Lieutenant."

There was distinct food for thought in that. No matter how far flung the tangents in the case appeared to be, they touched as a common circumference the enveloping influence of Mrs. Endicott.

"Is this girl still confined at the institution, Mrs. Siddons?"

"I don't know. There has been nothing said—no communication."

"What was the colour of her hair, Mrs. Siddons?"

"Black—the deepest, prettiest black I ever saw. They say that opposites are attracted to one another, and it was so in her case."

"What do you mean by that?"

"Her husband was a blond."

Lieutenant Valcour caught his breath sharply. It fitted surprisingly well—the motive—the crime—the fact that the girl might have retained her key to the servants' entrance and her husband have got hold of it. And her husband would readily enough have believed the talk about his wife and Endicott— husbands had a habit of doing just that. To the man's way of thinking, it wouldn't have been anything so ephemeral as a maternal grandmother who had driven his wife insane: it would have been Endicott.

Madame Velasquez's innuendoes against the true identity of anybody came back to Lieutenant Valcour with annoying force. What about Hollander? Hollander was a blond, and obviously of a different level in education and position than the Endicotts. And who had identified Hollander? Nobody. Endicott and his wife were the only two in the house who could, and Endicott was dead, and Mrs. Endicott had not seen Hollander at all, if her unbelievable statement were true: that she had not gone out onto the balcony and along it to the window from where the shot had been fired.

Suppose the man who had sat with Endicott had just been posing as Hollander but had been, in reality, the husband of this unfortunate girl. Suppose he had been waiting outside for an opportunity to reënter the house, had waylaid Hollander and forced his errand from him, had taken his driver's licence and cards from him and had shown them to O'Brian at the door to gain admittance. . . .

No—there still arose that fundamental question: what had the attacker been searching for among Endicott's papers? This girl's husband surely would have nothing for which to search, unless it would be for problematic evidence of his wife's infidelity, and that theory was pretty thin. . . .

"What became of this girl's husband, Mrs. Siddons?"

"He is a sailor on merchant vessels." Her gesture vaguely encompassed the Seven Seas. "Where he is, or when, is as indeterminate as wind and tide."

Lieutenant Valcour did not molest her extravagance. He refrained from pointing out that few things were determined quite so accurately, nowadays, as the tides or, for the matter of that, the winds themselves. He stood up.

"Thank you, Mrs. Siddons."

"Shall I go?"

"If you will be so kind. Later, perhaps, we will go into greater details concerning this poor girl's husband."

Mrs. Siddons feasted her eyes for one parting, blinding instinct on the bed. She stopped at the door and said, "You will never get them from me, Lieutenant. And I am the only person who knows; who even knows that she was married at all. She confided in me, and if it was her husband who did this thing you will never drag his name from my lips even if my silence should mean——" Her eyes became clouded and her thoughts confused. She wanted to say something magnificent, something splendidly fitting to the occasion which she interpreted quite sincerely as a divine act on the part of God, with that poor, frail little Maizie's husband as His instrument on earth. Even if her silence were to mean what? The words wouldn't form. They rattled around in her tired head meaninglessly: bar of justice—herself in the dock—oh, it was cruel—life was cruel, and living was crueler still. Only death was kind, sleep and peace beneath the shelter of His sweet omnipotence. She stumbled a little as she crossed the threshold and made her way, sobbing futilely, back upstairs.

# CHAPTER XXVII
## 5:46 *a. m.*—Mrs. Endicott Cannot Be Found

L<small>IEUTENANT</small> V<small>ALCOUR</small> stepped across the corridor and rapped on the door of Mrs. Endicott's room. There was no response. He rapped again, and still there was no response. He turned the knob and the door swung inward.

The room was empty.

He closed the door and called to Cassidy, who was at the other end of the corridor.

"Sir?" said Cassidy, when he had joined him.

"You've been out here all the while, haven't you, Cassidy?"

"Except when I went upstairs to get the housekeeper, sir."

"That's right, you did. Come inside here for a minute with me. There are some questions I want to ask you."

They went into Endicott's room.

"Sure, it's good to see the daylight again, Lieutenant. Will we be cleared up here soon?"

"I have a feeling that we'll be finished pretty soon now. Tell me, Cassidy, was it you or Hansen fired first at Hollander?"

"Lieutenant, Hansen and I have been disputing that very point. We all but came to blows over it, we did."

"Why so?"

"Because I claim it was him who fired the first shot, and he still has the audacity to say it was me who not only shot first, but shot two times before he so much as pulled the trigger."

"That," said Lieutenant Valcour, "is exactly what I wanted to know. You were both right and both wrong."

"Now, how can that be, Lieutenant?"

"Neither of you fired the first shot, because it was fired by the murderer over there at the window. You heard it, and thought Hansen had fired. Hansen heard it, and then heard your following shot, and thought that you had fired twice."

"That must have been it at that, Lieutenant."

"It was. The second thing I wanted to ask you about is Mrs. Endicott. She isn't in her room. Have you seen her about the corridor, or anywhere else?"

"No, sir."

"Then go and look her up. Ask the men downstairs if they've seen her, and if they haven't, look through the rooms on this floor and up above. When you do come across her, ask her if she will please come in here and see me."

"Yes, Lieutenant."

Cassidy went out and closed the door.

Lieutenant Valcour was beginning to feel very, very tired. He yawned elaborately, stared out of the window for a minute or two, and then sat down again at the desk. There was something that he had intended to do there when he had been interrupted by the arrival of Madame Velasquez.

What was it?

It wasn't connected with that wretched premonition of danger which was nagging at him with increasing insistence. But it was something just as intangible . . .

Elusive as a shadow . . .

Yes, that was it—the thing that he had forgotten: he had intended to trace to its source that faint scent which was so curiously reminiscent of some place—some thing. It had come, he remembered, from the aperture from which he had taken the drawer. He shoved a hand inside and felt around. Wedged far in the back was a crumpled letter written on heavy notepaper. He pulled it out, and the scent became more penetrating.

It came back to him quite clearly now. It was the same perfume that had drenched the note left by Marge for Madame Velasquez up at the apartment. He took the letter from its envelope, smoothed it, and then turned to the signature. Yes, it was signed "Marge."

A knock on the hall door interrupted him, and he placed the letter on the desk. Hansen came in.

"Yes, Hansen?"

"I have searched all the yards you told me to, sir."

"Well?"

"There wasn't any gun, Lieutenant, that I could see."

"Did you look through all the shrubbery? There are some evergreens down there that I noticed."

"Yes, sir, I looked through and beneath every one of them."

"All right, Hansen." Lieutenant Valcour studied the young man facing him for a curious moment. "You were at sea for a while, weren't you?"

"Yes, sir. I was with the navy during the war, and after that on merchant ships for a year or two."

"Would it be possible for a sailor to climb up onto the balcony outside this window from the garden?"

"I couldn't say offhand, Lieutenant. I didn't notice much about the balcony when I was down there."

"Then go down again and see what you think. Let me know whether it would be an easy job, difficult, or impossible."

"Yes, sir."

Hansen went out, and Lieutenant Valcour had barely returned his attention to the letter from Marge Myles when there was another rapping on the door. This time it was Cassidy who came in. Lieutenant Valcour dropped the letter back upon the desk and turned to him.

"Did you find Mrs. Endicott all right, Cassidy?"

"No, sir, I didn't."

Lieutenant Valcour felt strangely disturbed. He had half expected Cassidy to answer in just that way; the denial was nothing more than a fulfilment of the curious premonitions he had been experiencing of some subtle danger.

"Did you look in all the rooms?"

"Yes, sir."

"Question anybody?"

"Everybody, Lieutenant. There's no one has seen hide nor hair of her."

"How about the men at the doors?"

"Each one was at his post, sir. She didn't go out."

"Then in that case," said Lieutenant Valcour, "she must still be in."

The thought was both a bromide and a consolation. Nowadays, Lieutenant Valcour assured himself, people didn't vanish into thin air; it just wasn't being done. While concentrating in his mind as to the possible whereabouts of the unfindable Mrs. Endicott, his hands were mechanically placing the piles of letters he had assorted back into the empty drawer. He had shoved the letter from Marge Myles carefully to one side. Any reading of it would have to come later, after he had hit upon some logical explanation for this sudden move on the part of Mrs. Endicott.

"He must have been some stepper, Lieutenant," Cassidy said, eyeing with interest one disappearing pack of pink envelopes.

"Quite a stepper, Cassidy." . . . Where *could* she hide? And why should she? . . .

"Each one of them piles from some dame?"

"That's right, Cassidy—each one from some dame." . . . She wanted to get out of the house, one could be pretty sure of that, and go to the hospital to see Hollander. But how could she have got past the men at the doors? She couldn't. . . .

"It certainly does beat hell what some guys can get away with, Lieutenant."

"But it never does beat hell, Cassidy." . . . And Hansen had been out around the backyards, even supposing she had attempted anything so unbelievable as to scale fences. That was absurd. . . .

"It ain't all a matter of looks, exactly—no, nor money, either." Cassidy's glance toward the bed was but half complimentary. "I've run with lads that was one step this side of being human monkeys, but could they pick them? I'll say. They had sex appeal. How about it, Lieutenant?"

"Undoubtedly, Cassidy." . . . As for the roof, it was peaked and offered no passage to the roofs of the adjoining houses. One couldn't picture her, in any case, scrambling over roofs any more than one could believe that she would scramble over fences. . . .

"And the worst of it is with these bimbos that have it, they ain't ever satisfied."

"No one is ever satisfied, Cassidy." . . . There might be a way to the roof at that, from the attic . . . attic . . .

"Not ever with anything, Lieutenant?'

"Not really ever with anything." . . . Attic . . . and that curious look that one had had to interpret as exaltation. It couldn't be possible, but still—— "Stay right here, Cassidy!"

Cassidy gave a nervous jump. The words were sparks from flint striking steel. Lieutenant Valcour's sudden spurt of speed as he rushed toward the door was surprising.

A possible solution to Mrs. Endicott's absence had just come to him with rather horrible clearness.

# CHAPTER XXVIII
## 6:00 *a. m.*—Mist Drifting Through Mist

Lieutenant Valcour was out of the door in no time and racing along the corridor up the stairs to the floor above. Somewhere—somewhere was the entrance to the stairs leading farther up to the attic. Ah!—softly now, quietly, not to disturb or shock. Thank God the treads were firm and didn't creak. . . .

There was a window in the attic, at the garden end of its peak, not a large window, but big enough to permit the cold white light of morning to illumine the place grayly.

Mrs. Endicott's back was toward him, her face toward that window, and the light from it blurred softly about her silhouette of darkness. She had upended the trunk she was standing on, and it had placed her hands within convenient reach of the rafter about which she had fastened one end of a short rope. Its other end was coiled in a running noose about her neck.

Lieutenant Valcour measured the distance between where he stood at the top of the stairs and the trunk. He could never make it. Some board would creak. And yet, if he cried out, or spoke, if he failed in the proper choice of a word—in fact, the least thing that startled her would destroy her almost calm stance of fatalistic poise.

He took a penknife from his pocket and, slitting the laces of his shoes, removed them. Thank God her back was toward him, and the window was there with its square of light cut clearly in muffled grays—its light with which she seemed to be holding some private service of communion—that inevitable farewell with earth indulged in by each wretched soul before exchanging its conscious lonesomeness for the obscure and problematic company of the damned. . . .

He was very near her now, himself a mist drifting softly through mist. . . .

Whispering—whispering—he could hear her whispering—a thin flow of meaning rather than of words, sent from the grayness to that light beyond—sent through a little measured casement out into the immeasurable brilliance of eternity. Her hands were resting easily by her side; her body relaxed more and more peacefully in repose.

" . . . and if you're there, Tom darling, and Herbert, too . . ."

He could leap forward now and catch her if it were necessary, but better be safe, quite safe.

" . . . it won't be heaven, dear. They have no room for such as you and me in heaven. But when you come——"

His arms closed gently about her, and her body seemed to stiffen into steel. She relaxed at once, and then stared down at him incuriously. She removed the noose from about her neck as casually as she might have taken off a hat. He lifted her to the floor.

"There isn't any hurry," she said.

He knew that she was hinting definitely at the future, when he and the law were finished with her and she would be free to book her passage for eternity again without supervision or restraint.

"No hurry, Mrs. Endicott; nor any need, now."

The "now" dragged her sharply from the mists. She stared at him with penetrating interest.

"Mr. Hollander," he said, "will undoubtedly recover."

"Yes?"

The word was clipped from some inner store of ice.

"Doesn't that alter the surface of things, Mrs. Endicott—of your intention?"

"Why should it, Lieutenant?"

"I am sorry that you choose to continue evasive."

"I'm not. It is you who see things, read things in people that are never there."

"That isn't true, Mrs. Endicott."

"What is there further that you wish to know?"

There was no compromise, no yielding, and the hardness in her voice was very definite. She looked almost extravagantly capable, too, in the smart dark dress she had put on. She was, Lieutenant Valcour reflected, one of those rare women who always "look their best" no matter what the time is or the situation; who make a point of looking so even when quite alone, and especially so, he added, when committing suicide. But he was not deceived by her hardness. There were invisible forces working within her, still stirred into turmoil by that impressive emotional ladder she must have so recently climbed in order to arrive at the decision to take her own life. If he were ever to understand this complex woman he felt that he must do so now, while he and she stood where they were in their private world—a tight little sphere of shadows sifted with mists of sunlit dust—and before they descended the attic stairs to the routined environment of daily living. He decided to attempt to lead her by certain matter-of-fact paths that would end in quicksands.

"Why did you have the address of Marge Myles in your directory, Mrs. Endicott?"

She answered with the mechanical patience of an elder explaining some academic problem to a child.

"It was necessary to take her into account. As I have already told you, she possessed a certain standing—enough of a one to differentiate her from the other women whom my husband picked up promiscuously—and the time might have come when I felt it advisable to get rid of her. Not murder—you're too intelligent to misunderstand me—there are several ways one woman can get rid of another woman that are just as effective."

"Which one did you employ, Mrs. Endicott?"

"It wasn't especially nice, but I wasn't dealing with a nice woman. I employed forgery."

This caught Lieutenant Valcour a little unprepared.

"Forgery?"

"Yes. I added a postscript to a letter Harry Myles had sent me before he married Marge. Harry never dated his letters. This one was harmless enough, but there was a reference in it to the camp he owned by that lake up in Maine. The postscript that I added changed the whole character of the letter. It made it apparent that Harry very definitely feared Marge was planning to murder him. I gave that letter to Herbert about a month ago, when it seemed that his interest in Marge was becoming dangerously serious."

"Didn't he ask you why you hadn't produced it before?"

"Yes. I explained that I had just come across it in an old letter file that hadn't been gone through for years. I asked him whether it was too late to do anything about it—show the letter to some proper authority, for instance. Of course I knew what he would say."

"That it was too late?"

"Yes."

"But didn't he also ask you why you hadn't said something about the letter at the time of Harry Myles's death?"

"I pointed out that we were in Europe at that time and didn't hear the news until many months later, when we got back. By then the letter had escaped my mind."

"And did your action influence your husband's feeling toward Marge Myles?"

"It was beginning to. Things like that work slowly; they keep breeding in the mind until they become effective."

She had missed, he decided, her century. When the Medicis were in flower she, too, would have bloomed her best.

"Mrs. Endicott, what was your real reason for sending for the police last night?"

"I can explain that better by accounting for my movements between the time that Herbert knocked on the door to say good-bye and you arrived. Will that satisfy you?"

"I hope so, Mrs. Endicott."

"I shan't lie to you, Lieutenant. I shall tell you the exact truth. Roberts was in the room with me, fixing some disorder in my dress. I left the room shortly after and started down the corridor for the sitting room. Mrs. Siddons, my housekeeper—I don't know whether you've met her or not?"

"Yes, Mrs. Endicott."

"She was standing at the foot of the stairs leading to the floor above. She said she had something to tell me, and we went into the sitting room."

"That was just after seven o'clock?"

"Five minutes—ten—yes. Mrs. Siddons brought up the subject of a particularly despicable affair that my husband was involved in with one of our maids over a year ago. Shall I go into it?"

"It isn't necessary, Mrs. Endicott."

"The maid was married. Her husband was a sailor." Mrs. Endicott paused for a moment, and seemed to be sorting in her mind which facts she cared to present and which, in spite of her recent avowal of candour, she preferred to hold in reserve. "You have probably noticed, Lieutenant, that Mrs. Siddons is an abnormal woman. She is the most striking example of the religious-fanatic type that I have ever met. Her life is literally built upon the composite foundation of faith and duty which she believes all mankind owes to God. Her belief in direct punishment visited by God on earthly sinners is a fixed idea. And last night in my sitting room she told me that God was going to strike my husband and that His instrument would be the husband of that maid whom Herbert had injured."

"But if that was an act which she so obviously desired to see consummated, Mrs. Endicott, why did she warn you—anybody—about it in advance?"

"Religious fanatics, Lieutenant, scorn the idea that human agency can interfere with the workings of any divine plan. Things, for them, are ordained and are supposed to happen just exactly as they are ordained."

"But why did she warn you?"

"She came to tell me about it, she said, in order that I might be prepared for the shock. She has always sympathized inordinately with me over what she terms Herbert's ungodly actions. I asked her, naturally, to be more explicit, and I finally forced the admission from her that she had seen, or else believed that she had seen, the maid's husband that afternoon loitering about the street in front of the house. She went upstairs, then, to her own quarters. It seemed absurd."

"Then it began to prey upon you?"

"Indirectly."

"How?"

"In its possible relation to something else."

Lieutenant Valcour became intuitive.

"You are wondering now," he said, "whether or not you ought to tell me all about the tea."

"How did you establish the connection?"

"Between your having tea with Mr. Hollander yesterday afternoon and Mrs. Siddons's story?"

"Yes."

"It's rather simple, isn't it?"

"Is it?"

"Yes, Mrs. Endicott, I think it is. You won't deny, will you, that you very definitely impressed on Mr. Hollander that your determination to 'end it all' either by committing suicide or killing your husband was sincere? Mr. Hollander *was* the confidant for your secret confusions, sort of a proving ground for reactions. I've already substantiated that theory, both through Mr. Hollander himself and his friend."

"No, I won't deny it."

"And you believed that he would do something to prevent you from accomplishing your purpose."

"I suppose I did."

"And in your naturally upset state of mind last evening Mrs. Siddons's curious prophecy concerning the maid's husband taking his revenge made more of a genuine impression upon you than you cared to admit. You were subconsciously afraid that something *would* happen—that the sailor might really injure or kill your husband, and that Mr. Hollander, when the police investigated, would somehow become involved. There was even a possibility that worshipping you as he does, when he heard of your husband's murder he might give himself up to the police and offer a false confession in order to shield you. It has often been done, you know."

"You are right, Lieutenant. I did think exactly that. The muddle of the whole thing began to drive me crazy during dinner. I went down at seven-thirty and ate nothing. I don't think I stayed at the table for more than five minutes. I went upstairs and into Herbert's room, looking for something. I really don't know what—unless it was for some sort of physical confirmation of his aliveness by the things he owned. Then I saw that note on his desk. I hadn't the shred of a nerve left by then, and the note genuinely worried me. It was such a direct confirmation of Mrs. Siddons's story. I wasn't exactly panicky, but I felt as if things had got out of hand. I tried to reach Mr. Hollander by telephone, but he wasn't in his apartment. I began to picture converging forces: himself—the maid's husband—and Herbert as a focal point. I felt that something had to be done. Well, I telephoned the police."

"Why didn't you tell me about the maid and her husband when I came, Mrs. Endicott?"

"It isn't the sort of thing one would plunge into directly."

"You would have told me in time, then?"

"Certainly."

"And why," he asked quietly, "did you try to direct my suspicions against Marge Myles when, in view of your special knowledge, that maid's husband was the logical suspect? That's a little inconsistent, isn't it?"

She looked at him evenly.

"Do you always do precisely the proper thing at the proper moment?"

"Rarely ever, Mrs. Endicott."

"Well, neither do I. I don't think anybody does."

She adopted again that patient, explanatory precision of the teacher. "A person's actions or statements during any moment of great strain are dominated by that moment itself, rather than being any sane reflection of logical and contributory causes. At such times one clings to straws."

"Marge Myles was a straw?"

Mrs. Endicott shrugged. "Herbert had gone, as I supposed, to see her. I believed that whatever happened to him would occur between this house and her apartment, or at some moment during the evening while they were together. I'm not claiming that there was any sense to my beliefs. I wasn't feeling exactly sensible just then."

"And you would have been quite willing to have Marge Myles blamed for anything that happened rather than either the sailor or Mr. Hollander?"

"Oh, quite."

It was very convincing—her willingness, that is. As for her credibility, Lieutenant Valcour retained reservations. He started along another divergence.

"Why have you kept Roberts so long in your employ, Mrs. Endicott, when you must have known how deeply she hates you?"

Mrs. Endicott smiled with frank amusement.

"You've never kept a maid, have you, Lieutenant?"

"Hardly."

"Then you can't appreciate fully what I mean when I say that

Roberts is a good maid. What earthly difference does it make whether she hates or loves me? I'm hiring her services, not her emotions, and her services are excellent. I've frequently wished that someone in my successive chain of cooks would develop a similar passion. There's something so binding about it."

He felt that she was escaping him again, that her armour was swiftly undergoing repair. In the brightening light her face shone clearer. She didn't seem quite such an enigma, after all. Nothing ever was, he reflected, truly enigmatic in daytime. It was just a tired face, wearied by any number of things other than the lack of sleep.

"I wish you would trust me, Mrs. Endicott," he said. "I'm not a bad sort, really, and I'm not trying to trap you into admissions that would prove injurious to yourself. There are still confusions that have to be straightened out. I have been assured by Mr. Hollander that you were devoted to your husband. You personally imply that your interest in Mr. Hollander is purely that of a friend, and yet you address him in your notes as 'Tom, darling.' And there isn't any question but that he worships you. The situation doesn't fall under the heading of the eternal triangle. It's a hub, rather, from which radiate several broken and uneven spokes."

"Broken spokes." The phrase appealed to her in a tragic sense inordinately out of keeping with its flavour of triteness. But then—he had said so to her before, ages ago—the trite things were the true things. And that's just what Tom and Herbert and herself were. And the hub? Passion, she supposed, or perhaps a composite illusion of all the various derivatives of love.

"It's hard to resolve human feelings into the simplicity of A B C's," she said. "I can't just say I loved Herbert because I was married to him and because he was the first person I ever loved, or that no matter how many other people there may be later in my life I will always return to him in my heart, just because he *was* the first person whom I loved, and expect you to understand." She brushed with elementary strokes through fog in her effort to be explicit. "I love Tom Hollander, too, just as much as I loved Herbert. It isn't nice, but it's the truth. Love isn't a unit, a single emotion tightly wrapped up in one word. It's a hundred feelings and desires and any number of little human hurts that are longing to be made well again." A certain bitterness crept into her manner: a bitterness of revolt. "The whole wretched business is too stylized. It's quite all right to love your father and your mother equally; in fact, it's held wrong not to—exactly fifty per cent of your parental love must go to each. Brotherly love must also be reduced to proportionate fractions. The love for one's neighbours is presumably scattered into legion. But if a woman announced that this otherwise divisible quality is spent upon more than one single man——"

Her laughter wasn't very pleasant to hear. Lieutenant Valcour felt a little upset; there was something disturbingly reasonable in her attitude. Was it pure sophistry? Not really. There was a strong element of fact and truth running through it all. It was useless to parade before her the different *clichés* of what any universal acceptance of her implied philosophy would do to society. He imagined rather accurately the treatment she would hand out to them. And like most people who had got what they wanted, he didn't know even faintly what to do with it. He couldn't come out flatly and ask her if she was planning to marry Hollander, and apart from the insight it gave him into her character there hadn't been any special advancement toward a definite solution of the problem of who *did* kill her husband, and for what motive. Lieutenant Valcour began to feel that it was he who had landed in the quicksands rather than herself.

"You have been very patient with me, Mrs. Endicott, and very kind. To an extent I am beginning to understand you. We have arrived again, but perhaps with a surer footing this time, at our stumbling block. Before we attack it, I wonder if you cannot think of any reason why your husband should have joined you up here in the attic when he found you here yesterday afternoon."

Mrs. Endicott was still too drugged with abstracts to attend very kindly to the mechanics of detailed fact.

"Well," she said, "it wasn't to commit suicide. That leaves your other nine tenths, doesn't it?"

"You mean that he must have been just looking for something?"

"There's hardly any other plausible explanation."

"But does he keep things up here?"

"He may have. This is his trunk."

She moved off toward the window, disinterested in anything further that he might care to do. A complete lassitude drenched her, and she sunned it negligently in the light sifting down through dusty panes.

Lieutenant Valcour righted the upended trunk and raised its lid. There were some papers lying loosely in its upper tray. He studied them curiously until he came across a certain one that caused him to draw his breath in sharply. He folded the paper and put it in his pocket. Then he closed the trunk. His manner, as he approached Mrs. Endicott, was implacably stern.

"I want you to tell me," he said, "just where about this house you have hidden Marge Myles."

# CHAPTER XXIX
## 6:30 *a. m.*—As Is Mirage

Mrs. Endicott stared sharply at Lieutenant Valcour. She was suddenly tensely alert.

"I think," she said, "that you have gone mad."

"Do you still maintain the pretence that when you were on the sill of your window and looking toward your husband's room you saw nobody on the balcony?"

"There is no reason why I should alter the truth."

"I shall be as patient with you, Mrs. Endicott, as you have just been with me. Listen carefully to me, please, and I will tell you why it is I believe Marge Myles killed your husband, and why I think you have given her sanctuary after the crime by concealing her some place within this house."

"I've no alternative but to listen, Lieutenant. But you are wrong—absurdly wrong."

"We will start with the initial premise, Mrs. Endicott, that Marge *did* murder Harry Myles in that canoe episode on the lake. I know that she has been paying blackmail to her step-mother, Madame Velasquez, for a long while, probably since the time of the crime itself. Well, a woman of her type doesn't pay-

hush money easily; she makes very certain, first, that the black-mailer really has the goods on her. Which made it simple for your husband."

"Herbert? Are you suggesting the fantastic idea that Herbert was trying to blackmail her?"

"People are blackmailed into giving up more things than money, Mrs. Endicott. I'm not suggesting that your husband was after money, but I do suggest that to further some abortive purpose Mr. Endicott held the postscript forgery that you made over Marge Myles's head as a threat. I have just found that letter in his trunk, and it is now in my pocket."

"Abortive purpose—— Don't go on just for a moment, please—I'm trying to make it fit."

"It's something along the lines of cruelty that I'm suggest-ing—some special cruelty."

"Perhaps. Herbert liked to see things squirm. He was sub-consciously sadistic."

"He probably drove her pretty far, because she made up her mind to get that letter—he undoubtedly greatly magnified its importance as evidence to her—no matter at what risk to her-self. I don't really believe that when she came here last night she had any intention at all of actually killing your husband. What she wanted was that letter. Did you let her into the house, Mrs. Endicott?"

Mrs. Endicott smiled a bit acidly and kept her lips tightly compressed.

"Because if you didn't," Lieutenant Valcour went on, "she must have stolen a key from your husband. At any rate, she was in the house here and searching for the letter in Mr. Endicott's room sometime around seven last night. Mr. Endicott should have been miles away up at her apartment, according to appointment, and leaving her a clear field. She had planned the whole thing out pretty carefully, because she left a note for Madame Velasquez, who was due to arrive at the apartment for a visit last night. Marge implied in the note that it had been written after seven when, as a matter of fact, it must have been written considerably earlier and planted in the apartment either as an alibi or as an explanation to Mr. Endicott of her absence. It would certainly have sent him hurrying off to the Colonial in search of her. It wasn't successful, of course, as he was undoubtedly delayed because of the quarrel he had with you, and was here in the house instead of up at her apartment as she had expected he would be. Don't you see that it rather all fits in?"

"Quite. But I still fail to understand what possible connection it can have with me."

"It has every connection with you, Mrs. Endicott, because unless we can prove that Marge Myles fired the shot this morning that killed your husband it will be unpleasantly necessary to establish the charge against yourself."

"I am probably very stupid, Lieutenant, but it is incomprehensible to me why I should shoot my husband around two or three o'clock this morning because Marge Myles was searching for a letter in his room at seven last night."

"Consider the problem, please, as two separate crimes and follow it through on that basis. At seven o'clock last night we have Marge Myles searching the pockets of your husband's clothes in his cupboard. He comes into the room, and she finds herself trapped in the cupboard. He opens the door, and the sudden terrifying sight of her gives him a heart attack. She believes him dead and drags him into the cupboard so that his body will not be found until she has had a chance to escape. She hasn't returned to her apartment, you know, all night, so it's quite possible she has either taken flight or is in hiding some place in the city."

"Then I can't, as you have suggested, be hiding her in the house."

It was Lieutenant Valcour who now assumed the rôle of teacher, with Mrs. Endicott as his young pupil.

"Not under that supposition. But if she did escape from the house at that time, what have we left? You found the scrap of paper on which she herself wrote a hinted threat in an effort to divert suspicion, and the writing of which was inspired by the distraught mental condition she must have been in. You called the police, and we found Mr. Endicott. Your suspicions jumped unerringly to the man who was uppermost in your thoughts: Mr. Hollander. He, you said to yourself, had done this thing to save you. Consequently, when you learned that Mr. Endicott had been revived and was expected to make a statement, you shot him to prevent his accusing Mr. Hollander, and you arranged your alibi with considerable ingenuity by only pretending to have taken the narcotic."

"It makes quite a case, doesn't it?"

"Yes, Mrs. Endicott, quite a case."

"And the alternative? You did suggest that there was an alternative."

"That Marge Myles has never left the house at all. That she is still here. And this is what the prosecuting attorney will offer to the jury: that with your knowledge she got onto the balcony through one of the windows in your room, shot Mr. Endicott, returned to your room, and was hidden by you some place around this house."

"All of which is unfortunately negatived, Lieutenant, by the fact that it was my slipper you found outside the window, and not hers."

"The prosecuting attorney can alter the action of the scene to suit that, Mrs. Endicott. After Marge Myles got onto the balcony you were terrified at the thought of what you had become a party to. You made an effort to recall her, when the shots were fired and threw you into a panic. You dropped your slipper and got back into the room." Lieutenant Valcour became quietly persuasive. "Which of my two theories shall I believe? I can make you no promises, Mrs. Endicott, because any confession that has been given under an understanding that there will be an amelioration of punishment loses value in court. But I can suggest to you that if you choose to make things easier for justice the act may prove beneficial for yourself. There are more unwritten laws than the common one so generally known."

Mrs. Endicott looked at him queerly.

"You don't worry me," she said, "at all. Any course that I might take can have but a common, a desired ending. The method of achievement is utterly inconsequential to me, as long as the ultimate result remains the same."

She was mounted again, Lieutenant Valcour decided, upon her hobby which carried her along indifferent trails to death. The apparent strength of her obsession rendered any further efforts on his part futile. In the attic there was, for him, no longer anything of mystery or the beauty of shrouded things. It was an ugly, littered room peopled by a smartly turned out beauty who, like a petulant and spoiled child reaching for the moon, sought further mysteries in that life which beckons from beyond life, and by a tired, oldish fellow standing stupidly in his stockinged feet away from his shoes.

"Come downstairs with me, Mrs. Endicott," he said. "As soon as my men have thoroughly searched this house you will be formally charged."

# CHAPTER XXX
## 7:11 *a. m.*—The Criminal and
## Weapon of the Crime

LIEUTENANT VALCOUR was once more in his shoes. Even in their laceless condition they restored his confidence in the relative fitness of things.

Mrs. Endicott preceded him down two flights of stairs and to the door of her husband's room, which Lieutenant Valcour opened. He looked inside and saw Cassidy sound asleep, seated on the large mahogany chest by the window. And he did not blame Cassidy so much as he envied him.

"Cassidy."

Cassidy's sharp return to consciousness would have reflected credit upon the hero of any Western drama.

"Sir?"

"Put your gun back, Cassidy."

"Yes, Lieutenant. I must have dropped off for a cat nap."

"We can discuss that later. I want you to take Mrs. Endicott down to the entrance hall with you and leave her there in charge of O'Brian. She is under arrest."

"Yes, sir."

"After that, warn the men on the servants' entrance and garden door to keep on their toes. If anyone tries to get past them on any pretext whatever they are to stop him. Look up Hansen—he may still be in the backyard—and then both of you come back here. We will then search the house."

"Yes, sir."

Lieutenant Valcour went into Endicott's room and closed the door. It was getting to be a mechanical action with him that caused him to go to the desk and sit down. The perfumed sheet of notepaper, which he had twice been prevented through interruptions from reading, caught his attention at once. He read the letter through.

I don't believe you [it began, without any preliminaries], and right from the start I tell you I think you are a liar and a louse. Harry never wrote your wife no such thing, and even if he did it proves nothing anyway. Nobody can prove a *thing*. You think it is funny to scare me and if you do it any more I am going to show you just how damn funny it is. I am through with you just the same way that your wife is through with you and you are a nasty rat.

MARGE.

Not really, Lieutenant Valcour decided, an essentially nice person. He folded the letter and put it in his pocket to keep company with the postscript forged by Mrs. Endicott. It would serve ably in establishing a motive and help the prosecuting attorney to clinch the case. Just as soon, he added unhappily, as he had unearthed the criminal and the weapon of the crime. That criminal, he repeated softly to himself, who with her weapon was still at large about the house, unless his theory of the case was basically wrong.

And therein lay the danger, the source of that curious presentiment of impending menace which had gripped him at odd intervals throughout the night. Strange that it should possess him most strongly in this silent room. But wasn't that just the association of ideas? Endicott, dead on the bed over there, and the path of that death-dealing bullet cutting through that corner over by the other window. He sought relief from a return of it by a mental mopping up. It didn't do to linger on presentiments. . . .

There were those few little side issues to think about; issues that had puzzled him, but which did not bear any direct reference to the main theme. He felt that they were explainable without any further personal investigation.

It seemed obvious to him, for example, that the reason why Mrs. Siddons had gone downstairs with her bonnet on, when the sight of O'Brian by the front door had turned her back, was a desire on her part to get in touch with Maizie's sailor husband and warn him that the crime she thought he had committed had been discovered and that the police were in the house. She had told Mrs. Endicott that she believed that she had seen him loitering about the street during the afternoon. And Mrs. Siddons would never have questioned her own ability to walk right out and find him because, if it so desired, Providence would have prearranged a suitable rendezvous.

. . . They came from that corner, really: those definitely significant waves of warning, as insistent as the scent that had led him to find the letter from Marge Myles in the desk. But they weren't a scent, nor were they anything so definite as a letter. They were (the astonishing thought thrilled him disagreeably) *Marge Myles*—her personality—herself—inimical. . . . Nonsense, nonsense—the room was empty. . . .

He forced himself to think of the two little bewilderments

that had troubled him in connection with the thoroughly bewildering Roberts. That pregnant look she had given him—what had it really meant, more or less, than an intense urge on her part to erase any spell of fascination which Mrs. Endicott might have cast upon him, and to plant in its place the seeds of suspicion of Roberts's own sowing. It had been nothing more, really, than that.

Now of greater inconsistency had been Roberts's suggestion of Hollander as the proper friend to stay with Endicott; for Roberts assuredly had held a fantastic passion for Endicott—fantastic in that there was this abnormal interrelationship of his personality with that of her war-killed brother—and she had just as assuredly been convinced that a liaison existed between Hollander and Endicott's wife. There was but one solution: Roberts had never observed Hollander and Mrs. Endicott together, and she had hoped, should morning bring a meeting, that under the natural dramatic effect of the setting there might be some betrayal. A look, perhaps, was all she wanted to confirm her suspicions. And there could have been in her mind no thought of any real danger to Endicott from Hollander, for had there not been a nurse and two policemen close by on guard? Then later, when Endicott was well again, Roberts could have told him the thing which she had seen.

. . . Mental fingers, that's what they were, plucking at his nerves and forming dissonances that chilled him queerly. He *wasn't* alone—but he must be—the room was empty. . . .

He would think of that Mr. "Smith" who lived with Hollander. Did he fit in—beyond one solid thump on the head? Only as one of the myriad side issues that cling like parasites to the trunk of each major crime. One could suppose (with reasonable assurance that the supposition would later prove to be fact) that Hollander was in some genteelly illicit profession such as bootlegging, and that Mr. Smith drummed up Hollander's customers for him among the night clubs—incidentally relieving some of the more foolish of them of their jewels. Mr. Smith might well have believed, at that moment when Lieutenant Valcour went to the telephone in their apartment, that if Hollander's goose was cooked his own might be cooked, too, and a blackjack had then seemed the simplest expedient that would insure his fading swiftly out of the picture.

. . . The room was empty—the room was empty. . . .

As for the emotional jungle of warped and sunless growths through which Endicott, his wife, Marge Myles, and Hollander had all groped their illusion-drugged way to this unhappy end— that lay beyond the punishment or acquittal of earthbound law. The proper tribunal for that must be found seated within their separate souls. Lies—evasions—fetid depths . . .

But *had* she lied?

Had there truly been no one on the balcony, as Mrs. Endicott had said?

The shot had assuredly been fired from the direction of that window above the large mahogany chest.

Above?

Presentiments were banished before the lash of fact. The lid of that chest was *not quite closed.* And the object that was holding it open, for the space of perhaps a half of an inch, was the small black muzzle of a gun.

Lieutenant Valcour's hand moved indolently toward the upper left pocket of his vest, in which there rested a flat, efficient little automatic of small calibre. He knew what had happened— that owing to his stillness for the last five minutes the murderer had thought the room was empty and was attempting to escape.

His hand moved more quickly, but not quickly enough. The lid opened wider—eyes—a face—a little shock of alarm, of terror—all ever so much more quickly accomplished than told. The lid slammed up.

"Quit it, Lieutenant, and put your hands down flat on the top of that desk."

"You're Marge Myles, of course," he said.

He flattened his hands on the desk's mahogany surface and stared curiously at her sultry beauty as she sat on the rim of the open chest. Flamboyant, that's what she was, and terribly bizarre from the effect of a shingled ripple of bleached blonde hair above her Spanish night-filled eyes.

"You have put yourself in my way, Lieutenant"—her voice was as disagreeable as the clash of dishes in a cheap restaurant—"and I am going to kill you and escape."

"I see," Lieutenant Valcour said politely, "that you believe in threes."

"How?"

"Your husband, Mrs. Endicott's husband, and now myself. One—two—three. For the sake of symmetry it is a pity that I am a bachelor."

She enjoyed for a full moment of silence—luxuriated in it, really—the sense of power which she held over this man. She had always enjoyed the power exerted by her body, and it was refreshing to drink quietly for a while of this different sort of power, which, through the medium of the pistol held unwaveringly in her hand, controlled the services of life and death. She would shoot him soon. . . .

Lieutenant Valcour hoped that Hansen would not blunder.

He could see Hansen quite clearly now, all but pressed against the outside of the window just behind Marge Myles. So Hansen, he reflected, had found that there *was* a way to climb up onto the balcony from the garden down below. What a handy thing it was, at times, to have been a sailor. Lieutenant Valcour fervently hoped that—the usefulness of the rule having been accomplished—Hansen would promptly stop being a sailor and become a policeman. He couldn't, and didn't, expect that Hansen would shoot a woman down in cold blood, nor would Hansen dare to startle her by throwing open the window or crashing through its glass. Could Hansen shoot through the glass and knock the pistol from her hand? Maybe once, Lieutenant Valcour thought unhappily, out of every twenty times. And she certainly wouldn't refrain from pulling the trigger while Hansen practised twenty times.

"Tell me," he said, "how you ever managed to breathe inside of that chest."

"The back of it is broken." The casualness of the question had startled her into an answer.

"Your own back must be pretty well broken, too." Was Hansen, the idiot, going to smash the glass after all with the butt of his gun? Hansen was staring very intently at him, seeking advice. He all but imperceptibly shook his head in negation. "And what did you have in the paper bag you carried when you came here and from which you tore that scrap of paper upon which you wrote the misleading note?"

"This gun."

"You carried the gun in a paper bag?"

"I was smart, was I not? Who would think that in a cheap paper bag there was a gun?"

"Not even a disciple of the fourth dimension." Hansen was aiming now at her wrist. It was absurd—he faintly shook his head again. No—no! "How did it happen that Mr. Endicott had his overcoat on but you had his hat?"

"I wear it for a better disguise. I have the dust on my face—there is the hat—it fits well over my cloche. The effect is astonishing."

"I see, and so when Endicott came back into the room to get it he couldn't find it and thought he must have left it in the cupboard?"

"Yes—yes—you are a smart man, too."

"And you entered the house with a duplicate key which you had had made from one of Endicott's?"

"Dear heaven, yes—how else?"

It did not please her that her climax should come at a commonplace moment, when inconsequential questions were being asked and equally inconsequential answers being given. It was not bravura: the man was genuinely unafraid. And she wanted him to be afraid. One shouldn't just dribble from the world: there should be a blaze, a scene.

Then Hansen rapped, quite gently, upon the panes.

Inspiration? Genius? Perhaps. Lieutenant Valcour's Gallic blood swept back to the nation of its source and he could have kissed that dear, that brilliant Hansen upon both of his ruddy, his intelligent, his Nordic cheeks.

She whirled as if something had flicked her. Blue serge—brass buttons—a glinting shield. She pulled the trigger.

But the muzzle of the gun was in her mouth.

# CHAPTER XXXI
## 8:37 *p. m.*—Five Years Later

MRS. HOLLANDER thought for a moment of simply dialling the operator and saying, "I want a policeman."

It was what the printed notices in the telephone directory urged one to do in case of an emergency. But it wasn't an emergency exactly, nor—still exactly—was it a policeman she wanted. She wanted a detective, or an inspector, or something; a man to whom she could explain her worry about Thomas, and who could do something about it if he agreed with her that Thomas was in danger.

Mrs. Hollander wanted most of all a man like Lieutenant Valcour, who had so ably handled that wretched affair five years ago when she had been married to Herbert and Herbert had been shot. She wondered whether Lieutenant Valcour was still on the force, and decided to find out. She dialled Spring 3100. She grew nervous while waiting.

"This is Mrs. Thomas Hollander speaking," she said, when the same type of impersonal, efficient voice answered her as had been the one five years before. "I am 'phoning to inquire whether a Lieutenant Valcour is still connected with the police force. . . . I beg your pardon? Oh." She gave the address of her apartment house on Park Avenue.

"This is Mrs. Thomas Hollander speaking," she began again upon a second voice saying, "Hello!" "and I am trying to get in touch with a Lieutenant Valcour who——— I beg your pardon? . . . You *are* Lieutenant Valcour—Inspector, is it? But how perfectly efficient! I am worried, Inspector, about Mr. Hollander, and I wonder whether it would be possible for you to come up and talk it over with me. . . . No, he hasn't disappeared. I know exactly where he has gone, but I have reason to believe that something might happen to him. . . . Yes, I am the Mrs. Hollander who was formerly Mrs. Herbert Endicott. . . . Yes, that dreadful affair. . . . Oh, you will? Thank you so much."

Inspector Valcour smiled a curiously satisfied little smile all to himself as he sat in a department limousine, chauffered by a department driver, and sped smoothly north along Lafayette Street on the way to Mrs. Hollander's address on Park Avenue.

And he thought of many things.

He thought of Marge Myles and of Herbert Endicott, who were dead; and of Madame Velasquez who, too, had died.

He thought of Mrs. Siddons, returned to her native New England hills, sinking her body and her being into their granite harshnesses and drawing amazing sustenance from them, as a flower will that grows in the imperceptible fissure of some solid rock.

He thought of Roberts whom he had never seen again and of whom he had never again heard, after the violation of the Sullivan Law had been charged against her, and her sentence suspended. She had gone back to England, probably, to lapse into a proper background for her neurotic broodings.

And that partner of Hollander's—the Southernistic Mr. Smith. He had faded entirely, never to return; nor was the fact of any consequence at all. He had been at best a side issue too unimportant for further bother.

But most of all he thought of Mrs. Endicott, who was now Mrs. Hollander.

The annals of history and the annals of crime were fringed with women just like her: beautiful, astonishing women, who revolved with their uncertainties like satellites about the world of normal beings, trailing their baleful, striking brilliance like an impalpable poisonous gas across the surface of every person whom they plucked and tortured within the intricate enigma of their hearts. The law never could touch her—nor could a person, either. She would escape. She would always escape, with the subtlety of mercury slipping between impotent fingers.

For she *had* escaped.

There wasn't any doubt in his mind about that. She had been the focal point five years ago in that Endicott case, no matter what the law or men might say. Her forgery of that postscript had had a deeper, a more deliberate intention than the mere breaking up of any affair between her husband and Marge Myles: it was to have been a breaking up of all of his affairs. Of him.

She was the true murderer of her husband, and not Marge Myles. She had simply spread the powder train to a suitably lethal explosive and had then applied the match. The movements of the others had been nothing more than gyrations performed by stringed puppets. And she had held the strings. Some of her puppets had died, committed suicide, and been killed. And it didn't matter in the least. The world was ageless, she herself was ageless, and plenty of puppets grew perennially every spring.

Inspector Valcour wondered, as he descended to the curb and prepared to enter the lift to her apartment, whether Thomas had become a puppet, too.

## THE END

# DISCUSSION QUESTIONS

- Did any aspects of the plot date the story? If so, which?

- Would the story be different if it were set in the present day? If so, how?

- Did the social context of the time play a role in the narrative? If so, how?

- If you were one of the main characters, would you have acted differently at any point in the story?

- Did you identify with any of the characters? If so, which?

- Did this book remind you of any present day authors? If so, which?

*All titles are available in hardcover and in trade paperback.*

Order from your favorite bookstore or from
The Mysterious Bookshop, 58 Warren Street, New York, N.Y. 10007
(www.mysteriousbookshop.com).

**Charlotte Armstrong, *The Chocolate Cobweb*.** When Amanda Garth was born, a mix-up caused the hospital to briefly hand her over to the prestigious Garrison family instead of to her birth parents. The error was quickly fixed, Amanda was never told, and the secret was forgotten for twenty-three years ... until her aunt revealed it in casual conversation. But what if the initial switch never actually occurred? **Introduction by A. J. Finn.**

**Charlotte Armstrong, *The Unsuspected*.** First published in 1946, this suspenseful novel opens with a young woman who has ostensibly hanged herself, leaving a suicide note. Her friend doesn't believe it and begins an investigation that puts her own life in jeopardy. It was filmed in 1947 by Warner Brothers, starring Claude Rains and Joan Caulfield. **Introduction by Otto Penzler.**

**Anthony Boucher, *The Case of the Baker Street Irregulars*.** When a studio announces a new hard-boiled Sherlock Holmes film, the Baker Street Irregulars begin a campaign to discredit it. Attempting to mollify them, the producers invite members to the set, where threats are received, each referring to one of the original Holmes tales, followed by murder. Fortunately, the amateur sleuths use Holmesian lessons to solve the crime. **Introduction by Otto Penzler.**

**Anthony Boucher, *Rocket to the Morgue*.** Hilary Foulkes has made so many enemies that it is difficult to speculate who was responsible for stabbing him nearly to death in a room with only one door through which no one was seen entering or leaving. This classic locked room mystery is populated by such thinly disguised science fiction legends as Robert Heinlein, L. Ron Hubbard, and John W. Campbell. **Introduction by F. Paul Wilson.**

**Fredric Brown, *The Fabulous Clipjoint*.** Brown's outstanding mystery won an Edgar as the best first novel of the year (1947). When Wallace Hunter is found dead in an alley after a long night of drinking, the police don't really care. But his teenage son Ed and his uncle Am, the carnival worker, are convinced that some things don't add up and the crime isn't what it seems to be. **Introduction by Lawrence Block.**

**John Dickson Carr, *The Crooked Hinge*.** Selected by a group of mystery experts as one of the 15 best impossible crime novels ever written, this is one of Gideon Fell's greatest challenges. Estranged from his family for 25 years, Sir John Farnleigh returns to England from America to claim his inheritance but another person turns up claiming that he can prove he is the real Sir John. Inevitably, one of them is murdered. **Introduction by Charles Todd.**

**John Dickson Carr, *The Eight of Swords*.** When Gideon Fell arrives at a crime scene, it appears to be straightforward enough. A man has been shot to death in an unlocked room and the likely perpetrator was a recent visitor. But Fell discovers inconsistencies and his investigations are complicated by an apparent poltergeist, some American gangsters, and two meddling amateur sleuths. **Introduction by Otto Penzler.**

**John Dickson Carr, *The Mad Hatter Mystery*.** A prankster has been stealing top hats all around London. Gideon Fell suspects that the same person may be responsible for the theft of a manuscript of a long-lost story by Edgar Allan Poe. The hats reappear in unexpected but conspicuous places but, when one is found on the head of a corpse by the Tower of London, it is evident that the thefts are more than pranks. **Introduction by Otto Penzler.**

**John Dickson Carr, *The Plague Court Murders*.** When murder occurs in a locked hut on Plague Court, an estate haunted by the ghost of a hangman's assistant who died a victim of the black death, Sir Henry Merrivale seeks a logical solution to a ghostly crime. A spiritual medium employed to rid the house of his spirit is found stabbed to death in a locked stone hut on the grounds, surrounded by an untouched circle of mud. **Introduction by Michael Dirda.**

**John Dickson Carr, *The Red Widow Murders*.** In a "haunted" mansion, the room known as the Red Widow's Chamber proves lethal to all who spend the night. Eight people investigate and the one who draws the ace of spades must sleep in it. The room is locked from the inside and watched all night by the others. When the door is unlocked, the victim has been poisoned. Enter Sir Henry Merrivale to solve the crime. **Introduction by Tom Mead.**

**Frances Crane, *The Turquoise Shop*.** In an arty little New Mexico town, Mona Brandon has arrived from the East and becomes the subject of gossip about her money, her influence, and the corpse in the nearby desert who may be her husband. Pat Holly, who runs the local gift shop, is as interested as anyone in the goings on—but even more in Pat Abbott, the detective investigating the possible murder. **Introduction by Anne Hillerman.**

**Todd Downing, *Vultures in the Sky*.** There is no end to the series of terrifying events that befall a luxury train bound for Mexico. First, a man dies when the train passes through a dark tunnel, then it comes to an abrupt stop in the middle of the desert. More deaths occur when night falls and the passengers panic when they realize they are trapped with a murderer on the loose. **Introduction by James Sallis.**

**Mignon G. Eberhart, *Murder by an Aristocrat*.** Nurse Keate is called to help a man who has been "accidentally" shot in the shoulder. When he is murdered while convalescing, it is clear that there was no accident. Although a killer is loose in the mansion, the family seems more concerned that news of the murder will leave their circle. *The New Yorker* wrote than "Eberhart can weave an almost flawless mystery." **Introduction by Nancy Pickard.**

**Erle Stanley Gardner, *The Case of the Baited Hook*.** Perry Mason gets a phone call in the middle of the night and his potential client says it's urgent, that he has two one-thousand-dollar bills that he will give him as a retainer, with an additional ten-thousand whenever he is called on to represent him. When

Mason takes the case, it is not for the caller but for a beautiful woman whose identity is hidden behind a mask. **Introduction by Otto Penzler.**

**Erle Stanley Gardner, *The Case of the Borrowed Brunette*.** A mysterious man named Mr. Hines has advertised a job for a woman who has to fulfill very specific physical requirements. Eva Martell, pretty but struggling in her career as a model, takes the job but her aunt smells a rat and hires Perry Mason to investigate. Her fears are realized when Hines turns up in the apartment with a bullet hole in his head. **Introduction by Otto Penzler.**

**Erle Stanley Gardner, *The Case of the Careless Kitten*.** Helen Kendal receives a mysterious phone call from her vanished uncle Franklin, long presumed dead, who urges her to contact Perry Mason. Soon, she finds herself the main suspect in the murder of an unfamiliar man. Her kitten has just survived a poisoning attempt—as has her aunt Matilda. What is the connection between Franklin's return and the murder attempts? **Introduction by Otto Penzler.**

**Erle Stanley Gardner, *The Case of the Rolling Bones*.** One of Gardner's most successful Perry Mason novels opens with a clear case of blackmail, though the person being blackmailed claims he isn't. It is not long before the police are searching for someone wanted for killing the same man in two different states—thirty-three years apart. The confounding puzzle of what happened to the dead man's toes is a challenge. **Introduction by Otto Penzler.**

**Erle Stanley Gardner, *The Case of the Shoplifter's Shoe*.** Most cases for Perry Mason involve murder but here he is hired because a young woman fears her aunt is a kleptomaniac. Sarah may not have been precisely the best guardian for a collection of valuable diamonds and, sure enough, they go missing. When the jeweler is found shot dead, Sarah is spotted leaving the murder scene with a bundle of gems stuffed in her purse. **Introduction by Otto Penzler.**

**Erle Stanley Gardner, *The Bigger They Come*.** Gardner's first novel using the pseudonym A.A. Fair starts off a series featuring the large and loud Bertha Cool and her employee, the small and meek Donald Lam. Given the job of delivering divorce papers to an evident crook,

Lam can't find him—but neither can the police. The *Los Angeles Times* called this book: "Breathlessly dramatic … an original." Introduction by Otto Penzler.

Frances Noyes Hart, *The Bellamy Trial*. Inspired by the real-life Hall-Mills case, the most sensational trial of its day, this is the story of Stephen Bellamy and Susan Ives, accused of murdering Bellamy's wife Madeleine. Eight days of dynamic testimony, some true, some not, make headlines for an enthralled public. Rex Stout called this historic courtroom thriller one of the ten best mysteries of all time. Introduction by Hank Phillippi Ryan.

H.F. Heard, *A Taste for Honey*. The elderly Mr. Mycroft quietly keeps bees in Sussex, where he is approached by the reclusive and somewhat misanthropic Mr. Silchester, whose honey supplier was found dead, stung to death by her bees. Mycroft, who shares many traits with Sherlock Holmes, sets out to find the vicious killer. Rex Stout described it as "sinister … a tale well and truly told." Introduction by Otto Penzler.

Dolores Hitchens, *The Alarm of the Black Cat*. Detective fiction aficionado Rachel Murdock has a peculiar meeting with a little girl and a dead toad, sparking her curiosity about a love triangle that has sparked anger. When the girl's great grandmother is found dead, Rachel and her cat Samantha work with a friend in the Los Angeles Police Department to get to the bottom of things. Introduction by David Handler.

Dolores Hitchens, *The Cat Saw Murder*. Miss Rachel Murdock, the highly intelligent 70-year-old amateur sleuth, is not entirely heartbroken when her slovenly, unattractive, bridge-cheating niece is murdered. Miss Rachel is happy to help the socially maladroit and somewhat bumbling Detective Lieutenant Stephen Mayhew, retaining her composure when a second brutal murder occurs. Introduction by Joyce Carol Oates.

Dorothy B. Hughes, *Dread Journey*. A bigshot Hollywood producer has worked on his magnum opus for years, hiring and firing one beautiful starlet after another. But Kitten Agnew's contract won't allow her to be fired, so she fears she might be terminated more permanently. Together with the producer on

a train journey from Hollywood to Chicago, Kitten becomes more terrified with each passing mile. Introduction by Sarah Weinman.

Dorothy B. Hughes, *Ride the Pink Horse*. When Sailor met Willis Douglass, he was just a poor kid who Douglass groomed to work as a confidential secretary. As the senator became increasingly corrupt, he knew he could count on Sailor to clean up his messes. No longer a senator, Douglass flees Chicago for Santa Fe, leaving behind a murder rap and Sailor as the prime suspect. Seeking vengeance, Sailor follows. Introduction by Sara Paretsky.

Dorothy B. Hughes, *The So Blue Marble*. Set in the glamorous world of New York high society, this novel became a suspense classic as twins from Europe try to steal a rare and beautiful gem owned by an aristocrat whose sister is an even more menacing presence. *The New Yorker* called it "Extraordinary … [Hughes'] brilliant descriptive powers make and unmake reality." Introduction by Otto Penzler.

W. Bolingbroke Johnson, *The Widening Stain*. After a cocktail party, the attractive Lucie Coindreau, a "black-eyed, black-haired Frenchwoman" visits the rare books wing of the library and apparently takes a head-first fall from an upper gallery. Dismissed as a horrible accident, it seems dubious when Professor Hyett is strangled while reading a priceless 12th-century manuscript, which has gone missing. Introduction by Nicholas A. Basbanes

Baynard Kendrick, *Blind Man's Bluff*. Blinded in World War II, Duncan Maclain forms a successful private detective agency, aided by his two dogs. Here, he is called on to solve the case of a blind man who plummets from the top of an eight-story building, apparently with no one present except his dead-drunk son. Introduction by Otto Penzler.

Baynard Kendrick, *The Odor of Violets*. Duncan Maclain, a blind former intelligence officer, is asked to investigate the murder of an actor in his Greenwich Village apartment. This would cause a stir at any time but, when the actor possesses secret government plans that then go missing, it's enough to interest the local police as well as the American government and Maclain, who suspects a German spy plot. Introduction by Otto Penzler.

C. Daly King, *Obelists at Sea*. On a cruise ship traveling from New York to Paris, the lights of the smoking room briefly go out, a gunshot crashes through the night, and a man is dead. Two detectives are on board but so are four psychiatrists who believe their professional knowledge can solve the case by understanding the psyche of the killer—each with a different theory. **Introduction by Martin Edwards.**

Jonathan Latimer, *Headed for a Hearse*. Featuring Bill Crane, the booze-soaked Chicago private detective, this humorous hard-boiled novel was filmed as *The Westland Case* in 1937 starring Preston Foster. Robert Westland has been framed for the grisly murder of his wife in a room with doors and windows locked from the inside. As the day of his execution nears, he relies on Crane to find the real murderer. **Introduction by Max Allan Collins**

Lange Lewis, *The Birthday Murder*. Victoria is a successful novelist and screenwriter and her husband is a movie director so their marriage seems almost too good to be true. Then, on her birthday, her happy new life comes crashing down when her husband is murdered using a method of poisoning that was described in one of her books. She quickly becomes the leading suspect. **Introduction by Randal S. Brandt.**

Frances and Richard Lockridge, *Death on the Aisle*. In one of the most beloved books to feature Mr. and Mrs. North, the body of a wealthy backer of a play is found dead in a seat of the 45th Street Theater. Pam is thrilled to engage in her favorite pastime—playing amateur sleuth—much to the annoyance of Jerry, her publisher husband. The Norths inspired a stage play, a film, and long-running radio and TV series. **Introduction by Otto Penzler.**

John P. Marquand, *Your Turn, Mr. Moto*. The first novel about Mr. Moto, originally titled *No Hero*, is the story of a World War I hero pilot who finds himself jobless during the Depression. In Tokyo for a big opportunity that falls apart, he meets a Japanese agent and his Russian colleague and the pilot suddenly finds himself caught in a web of intrigue. Peter Lorre played Mr. Moto in a series of popular films. **Introduction by Lawrence Block.**

Stuart Palmer, *The Penguin Pool Murder*. The first adventure of schoolteacher and dedicated amateur sleuth Hildegarde Withers occurs at the New York Aquarium when she and her young students notice a corpse in one of the tanks. It was published in 1931 and filmed the next year, starring Edna May Oliver as the American Miss Marple—though much funnier than her English counterpart. **Introduction by Otto Penzler.**

Stuart Palmer, *The Puzzle of the Happy Hooligan*. New York City schoolteacher Hildegarde Withers cannot resist "assisting" homicide detective Oliver Piper. In this novel, she is on vacation in Hollywood and on the set of a movie about Lizzie Borden when the screenwriter is found dead. Six comic films about Withers appeared in the 1930s, most successfully starring Edna May Oliver. **Introduction by Otto Penzler.**

Otto Penzler, ed., *Golden Age Bibliomysteries*. Stories of murder, theft, and suspense occur with alarming regularity in the unlikely world of books and bibliophiles, including bookshops, libraries, and private rare book collections, written by such giants of the mystery genre as Ellery Queen, Cornell Woolrich, Lawrence G. Blochman, Vincent Starrett, and Anthony Boucher. **Introduction by Otto Penzler.**

Otto Penzler, ed., *Golden Age Detective Stories*. The history of American mystery fiction has its pantheon of authors who have influenced and entertained readers for nearly a century, reaching its peak during the Golden Age, and this collection pays homage to the work of the most acclaimed: Cornell Woolrich, Erle Stanley Gardner, Craig Rice, Ellery Queen, Dorothy B. Hughes, Mary Roberts Rinehart, and more. **Introduction by Otto Penzler.**

Otto Penzler, ed., *Golden Age Locked Room Mysteries*. The so-called impossible crime category reached its zenith during the 1920s, 1930s, and 1940s, and this volume includes the greatest of the great authors who mastered the form: John Dickson Carr, Ellery Queen, C. Daly King, Clayton Rawson, and Erle Stanley Gardner. Like great magicians, these literary conjurors will baffle and delight readers. **Introduction by Otto Penzler.**

Ellery Queen, *The Adventures of Ellery Queen*. These stories are the earliest short works to feature Queen as a detective and are among the best of the author's fair-play mysteries. So many of the elements that comprise the gestalt of Queen may be found in these tales: alternate solutions, the dying clue, a bizarre crime, and the author's ability to find fresh variations of works by other authors. **Introduction by Otto Penzler.**

**Ellery Queen, *The American Gun Mystery*.** A rodeo comes to New York City at the Colosseum. The headliner is Buck Horne, the once popular film cowboy who opens the show leading a charge of forty whooping cowboys until they pull out their guns and fire into the air. Buck falls to the ground, shot dead. The police instantly lock the doors to search everyone but the offending weapon has completely vanished. **Introduction by Otto Penzler.**

**Ellery Queen, *The Chinese Orange Mystery*.** The offices of publisher Donald Kirk have seen strange events but nothing like this. A strange man is found dead with two long spears alongside his back. And, though no one was seen entering or leaving the room, everything has been turned backwards or upside down: pictures face the wall, the victim's clothes are worn backwards, the rug upside down. Why in the world? **Introduction by Otto Penzler.**

**Ellery Queen, *The Dutch Shoe Mystery*.** Millionaire philanthropist Abagail Doorn falls into a coma and she is rushed to the hospital she funds for an emergency operation by one of the leading surgeons on the East Coast. When she is wheeled into the operating theater, the sheet covering her body is pulled back to reveal her garroted corpse—the first of a series of murders **Introduction by Otto Penzler.**

**Ellery Queen, *The Egyptian Cross Mystery*.** A small-town schoolteacher is found dead, headed, and tied to a T-shaped cross on December 25th, inspiring such sensational headlines as "Crucifixion on Christmas Day." Amateur sleuth Ellery Queen is so intrigued he travels to Virginia but fails to solve the crime. Then a similar murder takes place on New York's Long Island—and then another. **Introduction by Otto Penzler.**

**Ellery Queen, *The Siamese Twin Mystery*.** When Ellery and his father encounter a raging forest fire on a mountain, their only hope is to drive up to an isolated hillside manor

owned by a secretive surgeon and his strange guests. While playing solitaire in the middle of the night, the doctor is shot. The only clue is a torn playing card. Suspects include a society beauty, a valet, and conjoined twins. **Introduction by Otto Penzler.**

**Ellery Queen, *The Spanish Cape Mystery*.** Amateur detective Ellery Queen arrives in the resort town of Spanish Cape soon after a young woman and her uncle are abducted by a gun-toting, one-eyed giant. The next day, the woman's somewhat dicey boyfriend is found murdered—totally naked under a black fedora and opera cloak. **Introduction by Otto Penzler.**

**Patrick Quentin, *A Puzzle for Fools*.** Broadway producer Peter Duluth takes to the bottle when his wife dies but enters a sanitarium to dry out. Malevolent events plague the hospital, including when Peter hears his own voice intone, "There will be murder." And there is. He investigates, aided by a young woman who is also a patient. This is the first of nine mysteries featuring Peter and Iris Duluth. **Introduction by Otto Penzler.**

**Clayton Rawson, *Death from a Top Hat*.** When the New York City Police Department is baffled by an apparently impossible crime, they call on The Great Merlini, a retired stage magician who now runs a Times Square magic shop. In his first case, two occultists have been murdered in a room locked from the inside, their bodies positioned to form a pentagram. **Introduction by Otto Penzler.**

**Craig Rice, *Eight Faces at Three*.** Gin-soaked John J. Malone, defender of the guilty, is notorious for getting his culpable clients off. It's the innocent ones who are problems. Like Holly Inglehart, accused of piercing the black heart of her well-heeled aunt Alexandria with a lovely Florentine paper cutter. No one who knew the old battle-ax liked her, but Holly's prints were found on the murder weapon. **Introduction by Lisa Lutz.**

**Craig Rice, *Home Sweet Homicide*.** Known as the Dorothy Parker of mystery fiction for her memorable wit, Craig Rice was the first detective writer to appear on the cover of *Time* magazine. This comic mystery features two kids who are trying to find a husband for their widowed mother while she's engaged in sleuthing. Filmed with the same title in 1946 with Peggy Ann Garner and Randolph Scott. Introduction by Otto Penzler.

Mary Roberts Rinehart, *The Album*. Crescent Place is a quiet enclave of wealthy people in which nothing ever happens—until a bedridden old woman is attacked by an intruder with an ax. *The New York Times* stated: "All Mary Roberts Rinehart mystery stories are good, but this one is better." Introduction by Otto Penzler.

Mary Roberts Rinehart, *The Haunted Lady*. The arsenic in her sugar bowl was wealthy widow Eliza Fairbanks' first clue that somebody wanted her dead. Nightly visits of bats, birds, and rats, obviously aimed at scaring the dowager to death, was the second. Eliza calls the police, who send nurse Hilda Adams, the amateur sleuth they refer to as "Miss Pinkerton," to work undercover to discover the culprit. Introduction by Otto Penzler.

Mary Roberts Rinehart, *Miss Pinkerton*. Hilda Adams is a nurse, not a detective, but she is observant and smart and so it is common for Inspector Patton to call on her for help. Her success results in his calling her "Miss Pinkerton." *The New Republic* wrote: "From thousands of hearts and homes the cry will go up: Thank God for Mary Roberts Rinehart." Introduction by Carolyn Hart.

Mary Roberts Rinehart, *The Red Lamp*. Professor William Porter refuses to believe that the seaside manor he's just inherited is haunted but he has to convince his wife to move in. However, he soon sees evidence of the occult phenomena of which the townspeople speak. Whether it is a spirit or a human being, Porter accepts that there is a connection to the rash of murders that have terrorized the countryside. Introduction by Otto Penzler.

Mary Roberts Rinehart, *The Wall*. For two decades, Mary Roberts Rinehart was the second-best-selling author in America (only Sinclair Lewis outsold her) and was beloved for her tales of suspense. In a magnificent mansion, the ex-wife of one of the owners turns up making demands and is found dead the next day. And there are more dark secrets lying behind the walls of the estate. Introduction by Otto Penzler.

Joel Townsley Rogers, *The Red Right Hand*. This extraordinary whodunnit that is as puzzling as it is terrifying was identified by crime fiction scholar Jack Adrian as "one of the dozen or so finest mystery novels of the 20th century." A deranged killer sends a doctor on a quest for the truth—deep into the recesses of his own mind—when he and his bride-to-be elope but pick up a terrifying sharp-toothed hitch-hiker. Introduction by Joe R. Lansdale.

Roger Scarlett, *Cat's Paw*. The family of the wealthy old bachelor Martin Greenough cares far more about his money than they do about him. For his birthday, he invites all his potential heirs to his mansion to tell them what they hope to hear. Before he can disburse funds, however, he is murdered, and the Boston Police Department's big problem is that there are too many suspects. Introduction by Curtis Evans

Vincent Starrett, *Dead Man Inside*. 1930s Chicago is a tough town but some crimes are more bizarre than others. Customers arrive at a haberdasher to find a corpse in the window and a sign on the door: *Dead Man Inside! I am Dead. The store will not open today*. This is just one of a series of odd murders that terrorizes the city. Reluctant detective Walter Ghost leaps into action to learn what is behind the plague. Introduction by Otto Penzler.

Vincent Starrett, *The Great Hotel Murder*. Theater critic and amateur sleuth Riley Blackwood investigates a murder in a Chicago hotel where the dead man had changed rooms with a stranger who had registered under a fake name. *The New York Times* described it as "an ingenious plot with enough complications to keep the reader guessing." Introduction by Lyndsay Faye.

Vincent Starrett, *Murder on 'B' Deck*. Walter Ghost, a psychologist, scientist, explorer, and former intelligence officer, is on a cruise ship and his friend novelist Dunsten Mollock, a Nigel Bruce-like Watson whose role is to offer occasional comic relief, accommodates when he fails to leave the ship before it takes off. Although they make mistakes along the way, the amateur sleuths solve the shipboard murders. Introduction by Ray Betzner.

Phoebe Atwood Taylor, *The Cape Cod Mystery*. Vacationers have flocked to Cape Cod to avoid the heat wave that hit the Northeast and find their holiday unpleasant when the area is flooded with police trying to find the murderer of a muckraking journalist who took a cottage for the season. Finding a solution falls to Asey Mayo, "the Cape Cod Sherlock," known for his worldly wisdom, folksy humor, and common sense. **Introduction by Otto Penzler.**

**S. S. Van Dine, *The Benson Murder Case*.** The first of 12 novels to feature Philo Vance, the most popular and influential detective character of the early part of the 20th century. When wealthy stockbroker Alvin Benson is found shot to death in a locked room in his mansion, the police are baffled until the erudite flaneur and art collector arrives on the scene. Paramount filmed it in 1930 with William Powell as Vance. **Introduction by Ragnar Jónasson.**

**Cornell Woolrich, *The Bride Wore Black*.** The first suspense novel by one of the greatest of all noir authors opens with a bride and her new husband walking out of the church. A car speeds by, shots ring out, and he falls dead at her feet. Determined to avenge his death, she tracks down everyone in the car, concluding with a shocking surprise. It was filmed by Francois Truffaut in 1968, starring Jeanne Moreau. **Introduction by Eddie Muller.**

**Cornell Woolrich, *Deadline at Dawn*.** Quinn is overcome with guilt about having robbed a stranger's home. He meets Bricky, a dime-a-dance girl, and they fall for each other. When they return to the crime scene, they discover a dead body. Knowing Quinn will be accused of the crime, they race to find the true killer before he's arrested. A 1946 film starring Susan Hayward was loosely based on the plot. **Introduction by David Gordon.**

**Cornell Woolrich, *Waltz into Darkness*.** A New Orleans businessman successfully courts a woman through the mail but he is shocked to find when she arrives that she is not the plain brunette whose picture he'd received but a radiant blond beauty. She soon absconds with his fortune. Wracked with disappointment and loneliness, he vows to track her down. When he finds her, the real nightmare begins. **Introduction by Wallace Stroby.**